"Please—please..." Susi whispered,
"do not make me feel—like this."

His arms tightened and he smiled.

"Like what, my lovely one? There is no need for you to answer, because I feel the same."

"It is—not possible," Susi tried to say.

But even as she spoke the *Comte* put his hand under her chin and turned her face up to his.

"You are so beautiful," he said, "so incredibly, breathtakingly beautiful, but it is more than that. It is something I have looked for, longed for and begun to believe did not exist until I saw you."

Then he was kissing her again, fiercely, demandingly, until she felt the fire on his lips awaken a flame within herself...a fire that came from the very heart of the sun....

A SONG OF LOVE
A HAZARD OF HEARTS
DESIRE OF THE HEART
THE COIN OF LOVE
THE ENCHANTING EVIL
LOVE IN HIDING
CUPID RIDES PILLION
THE UNPREDICTABLE
BRIDE
A DUEL OF HEARTS
LOVE IS THE ENEMY
THE HIDDEN HEART
LOVE TO THE RESCUE
LOVE HOLDS THE CARDS
LOST LOVE
LOVE IS CONTRABAND
THE KNAVE OF HEARTS
THE SMUGGLED HEART
THE CAPTIVE HEART
SWEET ADVENTURE
THE GOLDEN GONDOLA
THE LITTLE PRETENDER
STARS IN MY HEART (also
published as STARS IN
HER EYES)
THE SECRET FEAR
MESSENGER OF LOVE
THE WINGS OF LOVE
THE ENCHANTED WALTZ
THE HIDDEN EVIL
A VIRGIN IN PARIS
A KISS OF SILK
LOVE IS DANGEROUS
THE KISS OF THE DEVIL
THE RELUCTANT BRIDE
THE UNKNOWN HEART
ELIZABETHAN LOVER
WE DANCED ALL NIGHT
AGAIN THIS RAPTURE
THE ENCHANTED MO-
MENT
THE KISS OF PARIS
THE PRETTY HORSE-
BREAKERS
OPEN WINGS
LOVE UNDER FIRE
NO HEART IS FREE
STOLEN HALO
THE MAGIC OF HONEY
LOVE IS MINE
THE AUDACIOUS AD-
VENTURESS
WINGS ON MY HEART

BARBARA CARTLAND'S
BOOK OF BEAUTY &
HEALTH
A HALO FOR THE DEVIL
LIGHTS OF LOVE
SWEET PUNISHMENT
A GHOST IN MONTE
CARLO
LOVE IS AN EAGLE
LOVE ON THE RUN
LOVE FORBIDDEN
BLUE HEATHER
A LIGHT TO THE HEART
LOST ENCHANTMENT
THE PRICE IS LOVE
SWEET ENCHANTRESS
OUT OF REACH
THE IRRESISTIBLE BUCK
THE COMPLACENT WIFE
METTERNICH THE PAS-
SIONATE DIPLOMAT
JOSEPHINE EMPRESS OF
FRANCE
THE SCANDALOUS LIFE
OF KING CAROL
WOMAN THE ENIGMA
ELIZABETH EMPRESS OF
AUSTRIA
THE ODIOUS DUKE
PASSIONATE PILGRIM
THE THIEF OF LOVE
THE DREAM WITHIN
ARMOUR AGAINST LOVE
A HEART IS BROKEN
THE RUNAWAY HEART
THE LEAPING FLAME
AGAINST THE STREAM
THEFT OF A HEART
WHERE IS LOVE?
TOWARDS THE STARS
A VIRGIN IN MAYFAIR
DANCE ON MY HEART
THE ADVENTURER
A RAINBOW TO HEAVEN
LOVE AND LINDA
DESPERATE DEFIANCE
LOVE AT FORTY
THE BITTER WINDS OF
LOVE
BROKEN BARRIERS
LOVE IN PITY
THIS TIME IT'S LOVE
ESCAPE FROM PASSION

BARBARA CARTLAND

1

A SONG OF LOVE

A JOVE BOOK

First Jove edition published May 1980

10 9 8 7 6 5 4 3 2 1

Printed in the United States of America

Jove books are published by Jove Publications, Inc.,
200 Madison Avenue, New York, NY 10016

ABOUT THE AUTHOR

Barbara Cartland, the world's most famous romantic novelist, who is also an historian, playwright, lecturer, political speaker and television personality, has now written over 270 books.

She has also had many historical works published and has written four autobiographies as well as the biographies of her mother and that of her brother Ronald Cartland, who was the first Member of Parliament to be killed in the last war. This book has a preface by Sir Winston Churchill.

She has recently completed a very unusual book called *Barbara Cartland's Book of Useless Information,* with a foreword by The Earl Mountbatten of Burma, Uncle of His Royal Highness Prince Philip. This is being sold for the United World Colleges.

She has also sung an Album of Love Songs with the Royal Philharmonic Orchestra.

Barbara Cartland to date has sold 100 million books throughout the world. In 1976 she broke the world record by writing twenty-one books and the following years she wrote twenty-four, twenty-one, and twenty-three.

She is unique in that she was one and two on the Dalton List of Best Sellers, and one week had four books in the top twenty.

In private life Barbara Cartland, who is a Dame of the Order of St. John of Jerusalem, Chairman of the St. John Council in Hertfordshire and Deputy President of the St. John Ambulance Brigade, has also fought for better conditions and salaries for Midwives and Nurses.

As President of the Royal College of Midwives (Hertfordshire Branch) she had been invested with the first badge of Office ever given in Great Britain, which was subscribed to by the Midwives themselves. She has also championed the cause for old people, had the law altered regarding gypsies, and founded the first Romany Gypsy Camp in the world.

Barbara Cartland is deeply interested in Vitamin Therapy and is President of the British National Association for Health. She has a Health and Happiness Club in England and has just started one in America where she had a selection of her own "Be Lovely" cosmetics, her Album of Love Songs, and many other things of unique and original interest.

Her book *The Magic of Honey* has sold over one million copies through the world and is translated into many languages.

"I am going with my Soul bewitched
For I have dreamed my life away..."

When I visited Provence this year, for the second time, I found it just as mystical, magical and entrancing as I have described it in this novel.

The beauty of the women of Arles, the wonder of the barren rocks of Les Baux, the eeriness of the Gorges of Verdon were exactly what I expected but I did not hear the nightingales.

In 1938 an author wrote:

"I have never known such a place for nightingales and I acquired the habit of writing to their voices. In the Cypress trees and in the thickets there are nightingales...I had never imagined that so many could be got together for the nightingale is a solitary bird and does not like the propinquity of its own species."

And what should the nightingale sing about except love, especially in Provence? I like the song in the words of Uc de St. Cinc, a 13th century Troubadour:

"To be in love is to stretch towards heaven
through a woman."

A SONG OF LOVE

Chapter One

1889

LADY SHERINGTON gazed out of the window onto the very formal garden at the back of the *Duc* d'Aubergue's house in the Champs Élysées.

She was thinking that Paris was far more exciting than she had expected it to be, especially in one particular.

As the sun shone on her fair hair she looked very young, in fact, far younger than she actually was and very beautiful.

It had been amazingly fortunate, she thought, that the *Duchesse* d'Aubergue had been a friend for so many years.

They had met the first time when Lord Sherington had taken her to a formal party at the French Embassy and she had been afraid that neither her gown nor her jewels would compete with those of the other guests.

The *Duchesse* had, however, singled her out and they had been friends all through the succeeding years. Now when she had specially wanted to come to Paris, Lorraine d'Aubergue had invited her to stay as long as she wished.

"How lucky I am!" Lady Sherington said to herself. "So very, very lucky!"

The door of the Salon opened and she turned quickly with an expectant look in her eyes to see the woman of whom she had been thinking.

Lorraine d'Aubergue certainly looked extremely *chic* as only a Frenchwoman could, and the elegance of her gown with its satin bustle and the touches of lace under her chin made Lady Sherington know once again that she could not compete with her French friend.

"Ah, here you are, Susi!" the *Duchesse* exclaimed in English with the merest trace of an accent. "I just wanted to say good-bye. I suppose you would not wish to change your mind and come with me to the Prince's luncheon? It will be a very impressive gathering."

"I am sorry, Lorraine," Lady Sherington replied, "but you know I promised..."

"I know, dearest, I am only teasing, although I cannot say that I approve of what you are doing."

Susi Sherington looked worried.

"Is it—wrong of—me?" she asked hesitatingly.

"Not exactly wrong," her friend replied, "shall I say a trifle indiscreet?"

She laughed and threw up her hands in a typically French gesture.

"But, *ma Chérie*, why should you not be indiscreet in Paris when the sun is shining, you are unattached and,—in love?"

Lady Sherington gave a little cry of protest.

"Lorraine!"

Even as she spoke the colour flooded up her pink-and-white cheeks.

"Of course you are," the *Duchesse* insisted, "and Jean de Girone is very much in love with you! But be careful, Susi, that he does not break your heart!"

"Why should you—say that?"

Lady Sherington had turned away to stand once again looking out onto the garden, now with unseeing eyes.

"My dear, I have known Jean for many years, as I have known you. He is the most attractive man in France, but the most unpredictable and undependable."

The *Duchesse* paused, then said in a different tone which was one of concern:

"You are not serious, Susi, in what you feel for him?"

Lady Sherington did not answer and after a moment the *Duchesse* continued:

"I blame myself, I should have made it clear when he first met you that he is a heart-breaker; a man who plucks the most beautiful flowers by the wayside and when they fade, throws them away."

Still Lady Sherington did not speak and the *Duchesse* went on:

"It is not only that. Now that Jean is free of his tiresome wife, he has to marry money."

"He—behaves as if he is—very rich!"

Lady Sherington spoke almost as if she was startled.

"He was," the *Duchesse* replied. "As long as the *Comtesse* was alive. But her father made sure that as there were no children of the marriage, Marie-Thérèse's enormous dowry should return on her death, to her family."

The *Duchesse* made an expressive gesture as she added:

"*Hélas!* For Jean this was a cruel twist of fate! To have the handling of a huge fortune and then to lose it because his wife loved God and not him!"

"What do you mean?" Susi Sherington asked.

Because she was curious she turned her face towards her friend again.

The *Duchesse* sat down in a chair by the window.

"It is very remiss of me not to have told you this before," she said, "but I had wanted you to have a wonderful time in Paris. So when Jean singled you out and danced with you all night the first time you met I knew how amusing you would find him. He is the best dancer I have ever known."

Lady Sherington moved towards a chair opposite her friend.

"Go on," she pleaded.

"I thought," Lorraine d'Aubergue continued, "that Jean would give you the fun you have missed for so long, could thrill you with compliments which he can pay more skilfully than any other man I know, and make you look as beautiful as you were when we first met."

She smiled a little wryly before she added:

"He has certainly done that! But, Susi, dearest Susi, I shall never forgive myself if, when it is all over, you are left unhappy and heart-broken as so many other women have been."

"I have not said that I am—in love with—the *Comte*," Susi Sherington said a little defiantly.

"You do not have to tell me in words anything that is so obvious," the *Duchesse* replied. "I saw it by the look in your eyes as I came into the Salon just now when you thought it was Jean arriving."

"Now you are—making me embarrassed."

"I just want you to be sensible," the *Duchesse* replied. "Flirt with Jean, let him make you feel that you are the only woman in the world, as he will do! But remember that to Jean love is like a very good meal: it is delicious, but when it is finished, it is very easy to forget when you have eaten!"

It was now Susi who made a gesture and it was one of protest.

"You make him sound—horrible."

"I have no wish to do that," the *Duchesse* said quickly. "I want you to enjoy your little flirtation, but remember that is all it must be."

She looked at the expression on her friend's

face and went on quickly:

"Already Jean's relatives, and there are a number of them, all very distinguished, are thumbing through the Almanach de Gotha to find him a suitable and rich bride. She will have to be very rich to be able to keep up the Castle Girone, which is the most imposing in the whole of Provence, and the most historical. Jean has told you about it?"

"He has not said—much about it."

"Good!" the *Duchesse* exclaimed. "That means that he is not as serious as I feared, because let me tell you that the one great love in Jean's life is his home, his estates and the history of the Girones which makes them one of the greatest families in France."

"I remember reading about Provence," Susi said. "The Troubadours, the battles, the Sieges by the invading hordes."

"That is all in Jean's blood," Lorraine d'Aubergue replied, "and part of his mystique which attracts all women like a magnet."

"I can—see," Susi said hesitatingly after a moment, "that I have been—very foolish even to—listen to him."

"*Non, non!* You must not feel like that!" the *Duchesse* cried. "Of course you must listen to Jean, of course you must enjoy being with him! There is no-one in the whole of Paris who can be more enthralling and more entertaining. I am only telling you this, Susi, because of the position you are in."

"I—understand," Susi said in a low voice.

"Thank you for—telling me."

The *Duchesse* sighed.

"How I hate to be a spoil-sport! But when you told me of the conditions your husband laid down in his Will, I knew it would be impossible for you to marry a Frenchman."

She paused for a moment before she said:

"Not that I am suggesting for one moment that Jean's intentions would be honourable, even if you could remain as rich as you are now. When he marries it must be to a member of the *Ancien régime* and of course somebody young who can give him children."

She sighed before she continued:

"The children he should have had long ago, if his wife had not been abnormal, a woman who should never have been married, who should have gone into a Convent as soon as she was old enough to take her vows."

"Then—why did she marry him?" Lady Sherington cried.

"Because Jean's father wanted a daughter-in-law, rich enough to keep up the Castle, and Marie Thérèse's family wanted the prestige of her being the *Comtesse* de Girone."

"I—I suppose I had forgotten that the French always have arranged marriages."

"But of course!" the *Duchesse* answered. "It is a very sensible arrangement and works out in most cases extremely well. It is just that poor Jean was unlucky. Or perhaps the wicked Fairy at his Christening was determined that his life should not be entirely a bed of roses."

"It certainly sounds as if she cursed him!"

"That is exactly what she did," the *Duchesse* agreed. "Jean had good looks, charm, intelligence, a family history which goes back to the Princes of Provence—and a wife who hated him from the moment that she walked down the aisle on his arm!"

"Is that—really true?" Susi asked softly. "I feel so sorry for him."

"So do I," Lorraine d'Aubergue said. "But remember, Susi dearest, he will marry again very shortly, and it will be to somebody rich and young who will adore him and because she is the *Comtesse* de Girone, will turn a 'blind eye' on the many other women who will succeed those who have been captivating his heart since he was old enough to know he had one."

The clock on the mantelshelf chimed the hour and the *Duchesse* gave an exclamation of horror.

"I shall be late!" she cried, "and the *Duc* will be furious! I promised to pick him up on my way to the luncheon."

She rose to her feet with a rustle of her silk gown, then she put her arms around Susi and kissed her.

"Forgive me, dearest, if I have cast a shadow on the sunshine of your day, but I have to look after you and although I am younger than you, I feel immeasurably older and, if it does not sound conceited, immeasurably wiser."

"I know you mean to be kind," Susi replied in her soft voice, "and I am very—very grateful for your—affection."

The *Duchesse* kissed her again, then hurried

from the room giving a despairing glance at the clock on the mantelpiece as if she thought she had perhaps been mistaken when the hour had chimed.

As the door closed behind her Susi Sherington rose once again to her feet to stand looking into the garden.

The *Duchesse* had been right when she said she had cast a shadow on the sunshine. Something now was missing; something which had been there before.

"Lorraine is right—I must be—sensible," she admonished herself.

At the same time she knew that never in her whole life had she felt as she had these last few days since she had met the *Comte* de Girone.

From the moment she had been introduced to him and had seen an expression in his dark eyes, something strange had happened within her breast.

It was a feeling that had intensified during the evening when they had danced together, then sat talking in a manner which made words seem unnecessary as they could understand each other without them.

'I suppose,' Susi thought now, 'it is only because I am so unsophisticated, so countrified, that I not only—believed everything he said, but felt he was different—very—very different from any man in the whole world.'

As if the very thought of the *Comte* conjured him up, the door of the Salon opened and a servant announced:

"*Monsieur le Comte* de Girone, *Madame!*"

In spite of her resolve to be sensible, despite everything she had heard the *Duchesse* say, Susi Sherington felt her heart leap in her breast and an uncontrollable excitement sweep through her whole body as she turned round.

Just for a moment the *Comte* stood looking at her across the Salon. Then as the servant shut the door behind him, he moved towards her with an unmistakable delight.

He was the most handsome, attractive man Susi had ever seen, and the expression in his eyes drew hers so that she could not look away from him, but could only watch him drawing nearer as if she was mesmerised.

Automatically she put out her hand and as he took it and she felt his lips on the softness of her skin, a little quiver ran through her.

"Is it possible that you can be more beautiful than the last time I saw you?" the *Comte* asked in his deep voice. "You are so lovely that I cannot believe you are real and not part of the dream I dreamt all night."

With an effort Susi took her hand from his.

"It is very—kind of you to—ask me to have—luncheon with you in the—Bois," she said in a tense little voice, "but—I think perhaps it is an—invitation I should have—refused."

The *Comte* was still, his eyes searching her face.

"What has happened?"

"Nothing—I—I was just thinking..."

"Somebody has been talking to you," he said. "When I left you last night you were looking forward to our little expedition as much as I was."

Susi did not reply. Now she was looking away from him, and his eyes flickered over her straight little nose and the curve of her lips before he said softly:

"Have you really changed your mind about me? Or are you trying, when it is much, much too late, to be sensible?"

This was the very word Lorraine had used and as Susi started the *Comte* laughed softly.

"It is as I suspected," he said. "Lorraine has been giving you a lecture on propriety and of course, on getting too involved with me."

"Lorraine—loves me," Susi said quickly, feeling she must defend the *Duchesse*.

"As I do."

Susi drew in her breath. It was impossible not to know when he spoke in that way, that something very strange swept through her body to make every nerve vibrate to the fascination of him.

"Yes, I love you!" the *Comte* said, "and we both knew what we felt last night. But I told myself it was too soon to put it into words and because, my darling, you were very innocent and unspoilt, I must not rush you."

Susi's lips moved, but no words would come from them and the *Comte* went on:

"Why should we waste our time in pretending and trying to hide what we both know is the truth? I loved you from the very moment I saw you, and I think I am not mistaken in believing that you love me too."

11

The soft and caressing way in which he spoke made it very difficult to reply, and yet with a little cry Susi managed to ejaculate:

"We—must not—you know—we must—not!"

"Why not?"

"Because . . ."

It was impossible to finish the sentence.

How could she speak of marriage to him when he had not mentioned it to her?

"Because we come from—different—worlds," she forced herself to say. "Lorraine says we must only have a—light amusing—flirtation."

"And do you think that is what it is?"

"I—I have never had many—flirtations, but—I feel that we should—not be talking as if what we—felt was—serious."

The *Comte* laughed and when Susi looked surprised he explained:

"I am laughing, my precious, because you are so ridiculous, so utterly and completely absurd!"

Susi glanced at him, saw the expression in his eyes and looked away again.

"Do you really think this is a flirtation between two people who have met at a dance and just want to have fun for a few hours, a few days, a few weeks?" the *Comte* asked.

"That is—what it—has to be."

"Because Lorraine says so? My dearest dear, can you really control the beat of your heart, the throb in your voice, the expression in your eyes?"

She did not answer and he went on:

"Last night we talked to each other and it did not really matter what we said because my heart was speaking to your heart of love, real love, Susi! We both knew it was something very different from what either of us had ever felt before."

"It was—different for me, but not—for you."

"Who is to know that except myself?" the *Comte* asked.

She did not answer and after a long moment he said:

"Look at me, Susi. I want you to look at me."

Slowly, as if she was afraid to obey him and yet was compelled to do so, she turned her head towards him and he saw her eyes as they looked up at him were very blue, worried and afraid.

For a moment they were both very still. Then almost as if they did not move but melted into each other, his arms went round her and his lips were on hers.

At first his mouth was very gentle, feeling the softness of hers, then he became more possessive, more demanding and instinctively they both drew closer, and still closer as their kiss became more passionate.

Only when the world seemed to have stopped breathing and there was nothing in the whole Universe but the strength of his arms and the wonder of his kiss did Susi free herself to hide her face against his neck.

"*Je t'adore, ma Cherie*, I love you! I swear that no kiss I have ever given has been so perfect, so absolutely wonderful!"

His voice was a little hoarse and unsteady.

"Please—please . . ." Susi whispered, "do not

make me feel—like this."

His arms tightened and he smiled.

"Like what, my lovely one? There is no need for you to answer, because I feel the same."

"It is—not possible," Susi tried to say.

But even as she spoke the *Comte* put his hand under her chin and turned her face up to his.

"You are so beautiful," he said, "so incredibly, breathtakingly beautiful, but it is more than that. It is something I have looked for, longed for and begun to believe did not exist until I saw you."

Then he was kissing her again, fiercely, demandingly, until she felt the fire on his lips awaken a flame within herself.

It seemed as if her whole body was alight with a fire that burnt its way through them both, and came from the very heart of the sun. . . .

An hour later, sitting under the trees in a Restaurant in the Bois, the *Comte* said:

"Now we can talk."

They had driven in his chaise saying hardly a word to each other but Susi knew her whole body was tinglingly aware of him.

Now at the small table she was aware that his personality vibrating from him made it impossible to escape his magnetism.

'He is so handsome, so overwhelmingly masculine,' she thought, and blushed at her very thoughts.

His eyes were watching her and because

through shyness she could not meet them she busied herself with taking off her long white gloves. As she did so, she saw the sunshine glittering on the gold of her wedding-ring and felt as if the very brightness of it reproached her.

Although after a year of mourning for her husband Susi had laid aside the mauve and grey gowns that she had worn for the last three months, something sensitive in her nature had hesitated at immediately reverting to bright colours.

Instead today everything she wore was white, her chiffon gown trimmed with a heavy Valenciennes lace which also covered the crown of her hat and decorated the white chiffon sunshade she carried.

With her fair hair, her blue eyes and her pink-and-white skin, it made her look very young and, the *Comte* thought, untouched.

He corrected himself and changed the word to 'unawakened.' He knew it would be the most exciting thing he had ever done to awaken to an awareness of love, this enchanting creature, who had done something very strange to his heart from the moment they had met.

"Now," he said aloud, "you can tell me all the unkind and untrue things Lorraine has told you about me."

"They were not unkind," Susi said quickly. "She was only worrying about me because, as you know already, I am very—out of—place in Paris."

The *Comte* smiled.

"If you believe that," he said, "then you have never looked in your mirror!"

Before Susi could speak he added:

"Yet I agree that in a way you are out of place, not because you are unsophisticated as you were thinking, but because you are so different from the women we met last night at dinner, and all the friends with whom Lorraine fills her hours and finds amusing."

"Why—am I different?" Susi enquired.

"Because, my darling," the *Comte* replied, "you are someone out of a fairy-tale, a 'Sleeping Beauty,' unawakened and waiting for a kiss to bring you to life."

He saw the colour creep up over her face as he spoke of a kiss and thought it was the most beautiful thing he had ever seen.

"If you blush like that," he said, "I shall take you away this moment among the trees and kiss you until neither of us can breathe or think of anything except each other!"

For a moment Susi could not take her eyes from his. Then she glanced around saying in a frightened little voice:

"P-please—you must not say such—things to me—here—not when there are people listening—and watching us."

"They are all very intent upon themselves," the *Comte* replied, "and we have to talk about ourselves, Susi, as you well know."

"Then we must talk—sensibly!" she said firmly, "and I think Lorraine would be—shocked that after we have known each other for such a short time, you should call me by my—Christian name."

The *Comte* laughed.

"It is impossible for us to explain to Lorraine or anybody else that we have known each other since the beginning of time, and all through the years we have been journeying towards each other until finally fate allowed us to meet."

"Do you—really believe that?"

Her eyes were like a child's listening to a fairy-story and the *Comte* said:

"I swear to you that I believe that because it is true. I have been looking for you all my life, and if you imagine that now I have found you I will ever let you go, you are very much mis-taken!"

"B-but—we have to..." Susi tried to say, "I mean..."

Once again it was difficult to put what she was thinking into words and the *Comte* put his hand over hers that lay on the table.

As he felt her quiver at his touch, he said:

"You must know that we will be married as soon as it is possible!"

Susi's eyes widened.

"M-married?" she whispered.

Then she took her hand away from his and said in a very different voice:

"You must—forget you—said that."

"Why?"

"Because there is—something I must tell you."

"I am listening."

It seemed for a moment as if the words would

not come. Then at last, not looking at him but blindly across the Restaurant, Susi said:

"My husband—was a very—rich man—as I expect—Lorraine has told you. I was—married when I was very young—and he was—very much—older than I."

There was a note in her voice which told the *Comte* what the discrepancy in their ages had meant, but he did not interrupt and Susi went on:

"My family—who were not well off—were delighted that anyone so—important and so—wealthy as Lord Sherington should have wished to—marry me. He was very kind and—generous to them—as he was to me—but when he—died last year his—Will was somewhat different from what—everyone had expected."

Now Susi clenched her hands together in her lap and for a moment it seemed as if it was impossible for her to go on.

Then with an effort she said:

"My husband—left me a very large income—but if I remarried I was only to have an allowance of £200 a year!"

Her voice died away and Susi wished that she could get up and leave before the *Comte* spoke.

She dared not look at him.

She could not bear to see that the expression on his face had changed, that the love which he had said was so real had gone and in its place there was something else; something she dreaded.

She had the feeling, because he was so understanding and sympathetic where women were concerned, that he would continue to compliment her, to flirt with her and he would try not to let her feel embarrassed by what she had told him.

At the same time an ecstasy and a rapture beyond anything she had ever imagined would have gone.

There was a little pause before Susi said:

"You must have the children—you were unable to have with your first wife."

The *Comte* smiled.

"I have thought of that too. Lorraine told me you were married when you were seventeen and your daughter was born when you were eighteen. As she is eighteen, that means that you are now thirty-six. We are the same age, my lovely one."

Susi looked at him wide-eyed as he went on:

"I have calculated that we can have two sons before I refuse to allow you to have any more children."

"Two—sons?"

It was difficult to say the words.

"It is a tradition of the Girones to produce sons, but if one is a daughter, then if she looks like you, I shall love her overwhelmingly."

Susi gave a little choking laugh that was half a sob.

"How can you—talk like this? How can you have—worked it all—out?"

"My precious darling, I told you that I love you."

"But Frenchmen do not marry in such a way, Lorraine said..."

"Forget Lorraine and listen to me," the *Comte*

interposed. "You belong to me, and nothing and nobody is going to stop us from being married. Because we have taken so many years to find each other, it is going to be very soon, and I have already written home to tell my Grandmother that we shall be arriving to stay with her in two or three days time."

"How can we—I mean . . ."

Susi's almost incoherent voice stopped suddenly. Then she exclaimed:

"Trina! You have forgotten Trina!"

"No, I have not forgotten," the *Comte* said, "and she of course, can come with us. I realise the reason you came to Paris was to collect her from School."

"But what will Trina think about you—and me?"

"If she is anything like as sweet and adorable as her mother, she will want you to be happy," the *Comte* replied, "and I think, my precious, we both know that I can give you a happiness you have never known in your life so far."

That was true, Susi thought wildly. At the same time she felt as if everything was swimming round her and it was difficult to think clearly.

Because the *Comte* had everything mapped out, because she seemed to have no say in what she should do or not do, he had made everything seem inevitable and yet at the same time frightening.

When she had come to Paris to stay with Lorraine she had made the excuse that she intended to collect Trina from the Convent.

At the same time, she was aware that she wanted to live a very different life from what she had done so far, but she had never envisaged for a moment that she might find another husband.

She had always seen herself as living in the Sherington Mansion in Hampshire with the Sherington ancestors frowning down upon her from almost every wall, and continuing in her position as 'Lady Bountiful' until Trina married and she moved to the Dower House.

Because Lord Sherington had no sons and there was no heir to the title, the house and estate had been left to his daughter with a proviso in his Will that unless Trina's husband had an ancestral name of greater importance than Sherington, her husband must hyphen his name with hers.

It was the sort of rather complex, pompous idea that only her husband could have conceived, Susi had thought, then felt ashamed of being disloyal.

The whole Will had been filled with instructions that people should or should not do so and so, legacies to relations and retired servants, gifts to old friends, and quite generous contributions to charities and organisations in which Lord Sherington had been interested.

The only person who had been harshly treated was Susi herself, and it seemed inconceivable when the Will was read by the Solicitor that he could have made it a condition of her marrying again, that she would go to her new husband almost as penniless as she had come to him.

She knew this had been laid down because he had been jealous not of her behaviour with other men, but of her youth.

During the last ten years of their marriage he had been crippled with arthritis, unable to move about except in a wheel-chair, and he had almost hated her because she could walk, ride and when the occasion demanded, dance.

They had gone to the Hunt Balls because he was Lord Lieutenant of the County.

Susi had known as she danced with those who asked her as a matter of politeness because of her position that her husband followed her around the dance-floor with his eyes, not admiringly, as some of the younger men did, but angrily and resentfully.

He was always particularly disagreeable on the drive home and the following days until he could forget that he had watched her dance while he had been unable to get on his feet.

It was this resentment and envy which had made him determined that if it was possible she would remain unmarried until she was too old to want another man in her life.

As Susi had listened to the Will she could almost hear him pointing out to her the advantages of remaining Lady Sherington—the grandeur, the comfort of the big house, the luxuries she would still enjoy when she lived on the estate, the horses she could ride.

And there would be carriages at her disposal, an army of servants, besides a very large income which she could spend as she wished, entertaining in London, travelling, having anything she wanted, as long as she did not share it with another man.

"I am still young," Susi had told herself the night after the funeral.

When she got into the huge comfortable double-bed in which she had slept alone for so many years, she quite unaccountably cried herself to sleep.

Looking back, she had forgotten for the moment that the *Comte* was beside her, his eyes watching her.

Then at last when she felt the silence between them was full of things that must be said, she managed to whisper:

"You know it is—impossible from—your point of view."

"That is for me to decide."

"No—it must be—my decision."

"Why yours?"

"Because I—have to think about—you."

"If you are thinking of me, you will want me to be happy."

"That is what I want you to be, and that means that your Castle which Lorraine says you love more than anything else, must be properly maintained, so you must have money."

"You think that is more important than love?"

"You—you have—loved many—times."

"I am not denying that there have been many women in my life, but do you imagine that what I felt for them was anything like the love I have for you?"

She did not answer but glanced up at him for a moment and he saw the bewilderment in her eyes.

"Oh, my precious darling," he said, "you are so unworldly, so innocent in so many ways. How can I make you understand that what I feel for you is completely and absolutely different from anything I have known in the past? There are no words in which to explain it, I can only show you, so that is why we must be married very quickly."

"And supposing," Susi murmured, "supposing when we are—married—and I am not agreeing that we should be—you find me—disappointing. You will have lost—everything."

The *Comte* smiled.

"I shall not be disappointed."

"How—can you be sure?"

"I am sure in the same way that I was sure when I saw you that you are the woman for whom I have been searching through all eternity."

There was something in his voice that made Susi's heart beat so quickly that she could not reply.

Then their food arrived and they tried to eat what the *Comte* had ordered.

After luncheon was over they did not immediately step into his chaise which was waiting for them outside, but instead they wandered away under the trees in the Bois until they found a secluded spot by a small stream and sat down on a bench.

Then the *Comte*, turning so that he was half-facing Susi put out his hand and after a few seconds hesitation she gave him hers. Very gently he unbuttoned and drew off her glove.

He kissed her fingers one by one, then her palm, making little thrills run through her so that her breath came quickly from between her lips and she felt her heart thumping in her breast.

"I love you!" he said softly, speaking both in French and in English.

Then as he kissed her hand again he said:

"You will come to Provence with me the day after tomorrow?"

"You are—sure that is—something I—should do?"

"I want you to see our future home."

"I am not agreeing that is what it will be. How can we—afford it?"

"As I have told you, we will manage, and as it happens I already have an idea."

"An—idea?" Susi queried.

"When I knew I meant to marry you, I began to think what we could do about the Castle, which is very big and entails a lot of money being spent on it. But it is so beautiful that I want it always to look its best, especially when it belongs to you."

There was a note in his voice which told Susi that Lorraine had been right when she said that the Castle was his great love.

She asked herself frantically how she could take it from him.

'If I do so, he will hate me,' she thought, 'because he will blame me!'

In her imagination she saw the ceilings falling in neglect, the stonework crumbling, the rugs becoming threadbare, the curtains torn and faded.

Could their love, wonderful though it seemed at the moment, survive the years when he would reproach her for having caused him to be unfaithful to something which was part of himself?

'I cannot—do it,' Susi thought.

Then taking her hand from his because it was difficult to think while he was touching her, she said, using his Christian name for the first time:

"Jean—I have something to say to you."

"What is it?" he asked.

He knew before she spoke from the tension of her body, the way her fingers were linked together, that what she was about to say was something immensely important at least to her.

There was a long pause before Susi said in a voice he could hardly hear:

"I—love you—but because I—love you I know that I—cannot hurt you—so I have—something to—suggest."

The *Comte* knew by the way her voice trembled that she was finding it hard to say the words that came to her lips.

He waited and after a moment she went on:

"It may be—wrong and wicked of me—but because you must not—spoil your home—or your future—perhaps we could be—together—without being—married."

The last words were spoken in a rush and now Susi's face, which had been very pale while she was speaking, was suffused with colour.

For a moment there was only silence. Then the *Comte* said in a voice she had never heard before:

"Oh, my darling, my precious, wonderful little love, now I know what you feel for me."

He knew as he spoke that her suggestion was one which his smart Parisian friends would have expected him to have made. But that Susi with her conventional background and her intrinsic purity, should have suggested it, made him know exactly what it meant for her to put it into the words.

He took both her hands in his and feeling them tremble beneath his fingers, he said softly:

"Look at me, Susi!"

She obeyed him, her eye-lashes fluttering, and he knew how shy and at the same time, ashamed she was of what she had suggested.

"I adore you! I worship you!" he said very quietly. "I want to kneel at your feet and kiss the ground on which you stand. Now I know that your love, my darling, equals mine, and it would be impossible for us ever to be separated from each other!"

He bent and kissed her hands one after the other and said:

"I shall always remember what you offered me, and I must refuse simply because while I want you and need you with my whole body, my soul tells me that what we feel for each other comes from God and without His blessing we would both feel incomplete."

"Oh—Jean . . . !"

There were tears in Susi's eyes and they ran down her cheeks.

Then regardless that someone might see them, the *Comte* put his arms around her and kissed away her tears before his lips found hers.

Chapter Two

"I AM very excited, Sister Antoinette!" Trina said as they drove away from the station in the *Duc*'s magnificent carriage drawn by two horses.

"I am sure you are, Trina," Sister Antoinette agreed in her calm, quiet voice. "But as the Mother Superior has always said, we must learn to control our emotions."

Trina flashed her a little smile and replied:

"That is difficult to do when I have not seen Mama for over a year. I am sure she will think that I have altered."

"I expect she will," Sister Antoinette said. "You are much taller, for one thing, and you are certainly not as thin as you were when you first came to us."

Trina laughed.

"I was 'all skin and bone,' my Governesses used to say, and especially just before I left England, because I had Whooping Cough that winter. What I needed was the sunshine which I found in France."

She spoke with a warm affection in her voice, then leaned forward to stare at the high houses they were passing. With their grey shutters that she thought were so characteristically French, she would have recognised them anywhere in the world.

"Is it really a year since you have seen Lady Sherington?" Sister Antoinette asked as if she was working it out in her own mind.

"Yes, a year and nearly two months," Trina replied. "If you remember during the Christmas holidays after Papa died, Mama let me go to Spain to stay with Perdita and in the Easter holidays I was in Rome with my friend Veronica Borghese."

"Of course! I recall that now," Sister Antoinette exclaimed. "You are really a much-travelled young woman, are you not, Trina?"

"I wonder if, as the Mother Superior hoped, it has made me wiser," Trina replied with a touch of mischief in her voice, "but it has certainly made me appreciate the world that I have seen so far. But I still think I love England the best."

"That is as it should be," the Nun answered. "After all, England is your home."

With a smile Trina sat thinking of the huge house in Hampshire in which she had been brought up.

Sometimes she thought it seemed rather gloomy and she could understand why her mother had pressed her to stay with her friends immediately after her father had died.

But there had been horses to ride, her dogs to follow her everywhere she went, and a hundred other things to do on the big estate that she had never found anywhere else.

"Now Mama and I will be together," she told herself, "and that will be wonderful!"

She felt a warm happiness sweep over her at the thought that now her mother could be with her far more than she had been in the past.

Then Papa had always wanted her to be with him, and Trina knew, even though he did not say so, that he disapproved of the way in which she and her mother would ride alone without a groom, go boating on the lake, or skating when it was covered with ice.

Mama was such fun, far more fun than any of the girls at the Convent even though she had many friends amongst them.

Now as they approached the Champs Élysées where Trina knew the *Duc*'s house was situated, she found herself sending up a little prayer that her mother would be pleased with her.

'I want her to love me, and I want to be just like her,' Trina thought.

The carriage drew up outside the front door and even as Trina stepped into the Hall a door at the other end of it opened and there was her mother.

"Trina!"

"Mama!"

As the two voices spoke together, Trina was running towards her mother and their arms were around each other.

"Darling Mama! I have been longing, simply longing to see you!" Trina cried.

"And I have been counting the hours," Susi Sherington replied.

She drew her daughter into the Salon, then as the sun coming through the window illuminated her face under the small bonnet she gave an exclamation.

Trina looked at her apprehensively, as Lady Sherington exclaimed:

"But you have changed, you have altered! Why, Trina, you are exactly like me!"

It was true. Trina had grown to the same height as her mother and the thin, angular body of the adolescent had developed until their figures were almost identical.

They had the same fair, corn-gold hair, the same gentian blue eyes, that seemed almost too large for their small faces.

Looking at her daughter Susi began to laugh.

"It is absurd! Ridiculous! We might be twins!"

"I cannot imagine anyone I would rather have as a twin than you, Mama."

Susi sat down suddenly on a chair.

"I am a little bewildered. I was expecting a child, but I find instead that you are very grown up, a young woman, and a very beautiful one!"

"You are paying compliments to yourself, Mama!" Trina teased.

Susi looked startled for a moment, then she laughed too.

"Oh, Trina, I have missed you so terribly all the time you have been in France, but it was rather sad and gloomy at home after dear Papa died."

"I knew that was why you told me to stay with my friends in the holidays," Trina said. "It is so like you, Mama, to be so unselfish. But I would really like to have been with you."

"I had Aunt Dorothy and Aunt Agnes to keep me company."

"Poor, poor Mama!" Trina said, making a grimace, and they both laughed.

"They vied with each other at disapproving everything I did," Susi said, "and that was why I came to France to meet you! They disapproved of that too!"

"I am sure they would disapprove of the *Duchesse*," Trina said. "Her niece who was at School with me told me how smart and witty she is, and how the invitations to her parties are sought by everyone in Paris."

"That is true," Susi agreed, "and she is giving a party for you tonight. All sorts of exciting young men have been invited to meet you, and I am only hoping that you have a suitable gown to wear."

"Do not worry, Mama," Trina replied. "When you told me to buy some clothes in Rome at Easter, I spent an absolute fortune!"

"I am glad," Susi said simply. "I like what you are wearing now. It is very becoming."

Trina jumped up to slip off her travelling-cape, then twirled round and round to let her mother see the very elegant bustle and the waist which the girls at School had said enviously could be spanned by a man's two hands.

"You have always had very good taste, Trina," Susi said, "but of course, I have been imagining you in little girl's dresses."

"I have a whole wardrobe with which to dazzle you, Mama, but we must still go shopping together. There are lots of things I want to buy."

Susi hesitated, then she said:

"There will not be much—time for—shopping."

"Why not?"

"Because we are leaving—here the day after tomorrow."

"Where are we going?"

Again there was a little hesitation before Susi replied:

"I have—promised to go and stay in—Provence with the *Comtesse* Astrid de Girone."

The way Susi spoke and the way she did not look at her daughter brought a questioning expression to Trina's blue eyes.

"Who is she? I seem to know the name."

"You will find the *Comtes* de Girone mentioned in your history books."

"I will look them up," Trina decided. "But tell me about the present *Comte*. Is he a friend of yours, Mama?"

At the mention of the *Comte* the colour deepened in Susi's cheeks and Trina gave a little exclamation.

"Oh, Mama, he is your Beau? How exciting!"

"You must not say such things," Susi said quickly. "This is not something I can discuss with you, Trina."

She rose as she spoke in an agitated way and walked across the room to the window as if she would avoid her daughter seeing her face.

Trina gave a little laugh.

"It is no use, Mama," she said. "You could never hide anything from me. Tell me about the *Comte*. Is he fascinating, and is he madly in love with you?"

"Trina!"

Susi looked shocked and at the same time, embarrassed.

Trina went to her side and slipped her arm through hers.

"Dearest Mama, I am not a baby, and although you sent me to be educated at a Convent I have been staying both in Madrid and in Rome where no-one talks of anything but love."

"You are—too young," Susi murmured.

"Nonsense!" Trina retorted. "You were married when you were my age and if you want the truth, I have already had a proposal of marriage!"

"Oh, Trina! Why did you not tell me?"

"It was not a very exciting one. In fact, I would not have married him if he had been the last man in the world! But at least I was one up on most of the girls at School who have not got further than receiving Valentines!"

"You did not tell them?" Susi asked in a horrified voice.

"Of course I told them," Trina answered. "It was a distinct feather in my cap and, as they had not seen him, they did not know how repulsive he was."

Susi looked at her daughter and shook her head.

"I do not know whether to laugh or cry," she said. "I was expecting to look after my baby daughter—to protect her—against the world..."

Trina hugged her mother.

"But, Mama, dearest, you have always been the one who needed protecting and looking after. I think I have known that ever since I was about eight."

Susi took a tiny handkerchief and wiped the tears from her eyes.

"Now, Mama," her daughter said firmly. "Tell me about the *Comte* de Girone and the real truth as to why we are going to stay with him in Provence."

Trina took a last look at herself in the long mirror in her bedroom.

"*M'mselle est ravissante!*" the maid who had been attending her exclaimed.

"*Merci,*" Trina answered. "I do not think I need be afraid in this gown, of feeling completely eclipsed by the Parisian creations."

It was certainly very attractive and exceedingly becoming to Trina.

It was white, because she had been told that as a débutante that was the colour she must wear, the tulle which encircled her shoulders and cascaded from her tiny waist was like clouds touched with rain-drops.

Thousands of diamanté pieces were sewn on the transparent material which glittered and shimmered with every move she made.

The gown was a perfect foil for her mother's: tonight Susi wished, as she said, to look like a Dowager chaperoning her débutante daughter; she was wearing mauve.

Of all the gowns she had chosen when she was in mourning this had been too elaborate for her to wear and brave the disapproval of her late husband's sisters.

But now she had brought it to Paris and she had known that worn with the diamonds that were part of the Sherington collection, it made her look like a violet greeting the spring after the dark, cold days of winter.

"You look lovely, Mama, perfectly lovely!" Trina exclaimed.

"So do you, my dearest," Susi replied. "Oh, Trina, I am so proud of you, and the *Duchesse* says you will take Paris by storm!"

"I hope so!" Trina said complacently. "After all the polish I have been getting for myself this past year, it will be very lowering if nobody notices me."

"Polish?" Susi queried.

"That is what you told me I should acquire when we discussed my going to a French School."

Susi laughed.

"I thought it was a ridiculous word, yet now I think it is the right one."

"Of course it is the right one," Trina agreed, "and I feel exactly like a door-knocker that has been polished until it is gleaming, bright and inviting. But the question is who will raise it and knock?"

"Trina!"

Susi was half-shocked, half-amused by the things her daughter said.

Then they had reached the Salon and she knew that she was tense as they walked together into the room.

All the time she had been dressing Susi had been wondering what Jean would think of Trina and Trina of Jean.

She had, she told herself, so stupidly thought of her daughter as the child she had been when she last saw her, but she could not help wondering if things would be changed now that Trina was obviously a grown up, somewhat self-assured young woman.

There seemed to be a great number of people in the Salon and for the moment their faces swam in front of Susi's eyes.

Then the *Comte* was beside her and at the sound of his voice her heart as usual, turned a dozen somersaults.

He lifted her hand to his lips.

"I have never seen you in that colour before," he said in a voice that only she could hear. "It enchants me!"

Because it was difficult to think of anything but the touch of his hand on hers and his closeness which made her quiver, it was an effort for Susi to say:

"I—want you to—meet Trina."

She turned towards her daughter saying in what she tried to make a conventional tone:

"Trina, may I present the *Comte* de Girone."

As she spoke she saw the surprise in the *Comte*'s eyes and the flashing smile with which Trina greeted him.

"But it is incredible!" he said, looking first at Trina, then at Susi. "Completely incredible! You might be twins!"

"That is exactly what I said to Mama when I arrived," Trina laughed.

It was then that another thought came to Susi; a thought that was so painful it was as if a dagger pierced her breast and she told herself she had been extremely stupid not to have thought of it before.

But of course, that would be the solution to the problems that concerned Jean. . . .

"It was absurdly extravagant of you," Susi said.

"What was?" the *Comte* enquired.

"To have your own special carriage attached to the train."

"But I always have one when I go from Paris to Arles."

He spoke casually but they both knew they

were thinking that in the past it would have been easy because such luxuries were paid for by his wife's money which was no longer there.

"Besides," the *Comte* went on, "I want you and Trina to enjoy every moment of your visit to my home, and first impressions are very important."

"Yes, very," Susi agreed.

She was thinking of the surprise and what she thought was an expression of delight in his eyes when he had first seen Trina, and she thought that perhaps as time went by, it would be easier to think of them together and not so excruciatingly painful as it was at the moment.

Every instinct in her mind and body had told her the night after the *Duchesse*'s party that she would be wise to leave immediately for England and take Trina with her.

It would be difficult for Jean to follow them unless she specially invited him, but if they went anywhere in Europe she was sure he would turn up whatever she might say to try to prevent it.

Then she told herself she must not run away and, if he loved Trina as she was sure he would, then she must be content with his happiness because love was worth the sacrifice of self.

At the same time, it was something she had never envisaged that Trina should look exactly as she had done when Lord Sherington had seen her at her first Ball and three days later asked for her hand in marriage.

She had been astonished when her father told

her that he was not only delighted at the idea of her marrying anyone so distinguished but had already given his consent.

If Susi made any protests they had not been listened to. Besides she was not really certain what she felt herself about marrying Lord Sherington or anyone else.

She only knew that he seemed very awe-inspiring and very old.

After all at fifty, he had lived more than half his life while hers, she felt, had only just begun.

There had been letters, flowers, expensive presents. In fact, as her mother had said: "He is completely enamoured of you."

She had always been kept strictly in the School-Room and had enjoyed no social life until this moment, so it was fascinating to realise that she was looked at with envy by her friends and be told over and over again that she was making an outstandingly brilliant marriage.

Once they were married she met very few men and women of her own age.

It was Lord Sherington's contemporaries who were entertained to dinner, who came to stay for the big pheasant shoots at Sherington Park and who would then ask them back to house-parties in Yorkshire and Scotland, and invite them to stay for the classic race-meetings like Ascot and the Derby.

Although the men complimented her and called her a 'pretty little thing' and squeezed her hand when they said goodnight, their wives treated her as if she was still in the School-Room.

When Trina was born Lord Sherington began to talk incessantly about having a son, but then he began to suffer from ill-health.

First it was bronchitis which made him little better than an invalid during the winter months, then arthritis prevented him from enjoying the sports that had been so much a part of his life.

Susi became nurse to a fretful and often disagreeable invalid, but worse than anything else, entertainment of any sort became more and more rare.

It was then Susi found she could escape from her husband's querulous, complaining voice only in the Nursery where she could laugh and play with Trina.

As soon as she was old enough Susi took her away on her own from Nanny's disapproving eyes and they would go for walks in the wood or drive in a pony-cart without a groom.

As the years passed there were a thousand other things which were fun simply because they were both young, could laugh and talk nonsense, when there was no-one else there to look down their noses at Susi for not being more dignified.

Of course there had been no question of her ever thinking of love until a few days ago—or was it a few centuries?—when she had first met Jean de Girone.

"Why should he have this strange effect on me?" Susi asked herself.

She looked at him sitting opposite her in the

comfortable armchair in the travelling Drawing-Room, so debonair and at the same time, so masterful.

She met his eyes and felt the usual quiver run through her, while every nerve responded to him and she longed in what she thought was a very reprehensible manner to be close in his arms.

Because she felt shy she looked to where on the other side of the compartment Trina was reading a magazine.

"Why are you sitting so far away, Trina?" Susi asked. "Come and talk to the *Comte*."

"I am quite happy where I am," Trina replied, "and I promise to be a most self-effacing gooseberry!"

"I do not want you to be anything of the sort!" Susi said almost crossly, "and you are not to say things like that!"

"Why not, when they are true?"

Trina buried herself once again in her magazine and the *Comte* with a smile in his eyes, said quietly:

"Your daughter has tact."

"But I want you to get to know each other."

"There is plenty of time for that, and at the moment I want to talk to you."

"What about?"

The *Comte* moved to sit next to Susi so as to make it impossible for Trina to hear what he said.

"You have told her about us?" he asked.

Susi did not answer and he waited. She felt that he was willing her to reply whether she wished to do so or not.

"N-not—exactly," she said at length, "but she—guessed."

"She would have been very obtuse not to realise that I love you," the *Comte* said, "and that you love me."

Susi made a little gesture as if she would repudiate the idea, and after a moment he said:

"You have not changed your mind, have you, Susi? I thought last night that somehow there was a barrier between us. I was not certain what it was, but I felt it was there."

"I have—told you that what you have—suggested is—impossible."

"We cannot go over that again," the *Comte* said. "Stop thinking about me and think about yourself. I know what your life has been like until now, and I intend to change it, and completely."

Susi thought if that was possible it would be the most wonderful thing that could ever happen, but she told herself she had to be strong, she had to save him from himself.

If he married Trina, then at least she could see him and hear his voice.

Somewhere, far away at the back of her mind there was a question of whether that would be enough, but she refused to consider it.

Trina, with her great fortune and being so young, was exactly what Jean needed in a wife, and what Castle Girone needed too.

Then as if he knew she was thinking of his home the *Comte* began to talk about it.

"I have been thinking all night of how exciting it will be to show you where I was brought up and where much of the history of Provence was enacted."

He had raised his voice, and now Trina was listening too.

"Is your Castle very old?" she asked.

"Parts of it were there at the time of the Romans," the *Comte* replied, "but what will amuse you most are the strange innovations introduced by my great, great, great-grandfather."

"Who was he?"

"He was *Comte* Bernhard, one of the legendary characters of Provence, an eccentric, a man who will never be forgotten, mostly because magical powers were attributed to him."

"Magical!" Trina exclaimed. "In what way?"

The *Comte* smiled.

"When you have been in Provence for sometime you will find that they speak of some people as *fadas*."

"What are they?" Trina enquired.

"They are really visionaries, the painters, the poets, the bewitched who believe in fairies, who see the Virgin in a tree's foliage, and who can predict the future."

"Like the Scottish who are fey," Trina remarked.

"Exactly!" the *Comte* agreed, "and actually the word *fada* comes from *fata*—the fay!"

"And that was what your ancestor was?"

"What everybody believed him to be. But I

think, as a matter of fact, he was a bit of a hypocrite."

"Why?" Trina enquired.

She had crossed the carriage now and was sitting as Susi had wanted near to them, a rapt expression on her face, as she listened to the *Comte*.

"My great, great, great-grandfather was an inventor very much ahead of his time," the *Comte* explained. "During his life there was a great deal of strife amongst the different families of Provence and they were continually engaged in battles with the rest of France."

"I remember that their armies were always crossing the Var," Trina cried.

"Exactly!" the *Comte* agreed. "And it was then Bernhard, who knew of the secret passages which were already in the Castle, contrived some more ingenious ones of his own."

"What were they like?" Trina asked.

"There was hardly a main room in the whole building in which it was not possible for him to disappear at a moment's notice."

"How thrilling!" Trina exclaimed, and the *Comte* realised that Susi too was listening with shining eyes.

"He brought craftsmen from Italy, men who were past-masters at that sort of work. You can touch a mantelpiece and it turns round completely, a lever moves a stone in the wall and in a moment it is impossible for anyone to know that you have ever been in the room you have just left."

"Go on," Trina cried as the *Comte* paused.

"There are small staircases hidden in turrets," he continued, "by which you can go from the roof to dungeons without even setting foot in any other part of the Castle."

"It is the most exciting thing I have ever heard," Trina cried. "Will you show them to us?"

"I will show you those I know about," the *Comte* replied. "As a matter of fact, I am told there are a great many still undiscovered, or rather forgotten over the ages."

"And the people thought," Susi said, "that the *Comte* Bernhard was a magician."

"They thought he had the wings of angels and the cunning of the Devil," the *Comte* replied. "Time after time his enemies stormed the Castle certain he was inside, and yet although they searched it with a whole army of soldiers, they never discovered him."

He laughed as he went on:

"Sometimes he would taunt them from the battlements, and when a hundred archers aimed their arrows at him, they would hear him laughing from lower down near the moat."

"Is there a moat?" Trina enquired.

"In the front of the Castle," the *Comte* replied, "and a draw-bridge."

"It is the sort of Castle I have always dreamt of visiting," she said, "and I am sure it is like the ones Mama described in the fairy-stories she used to tell me when I was a little girl."

"I have already told your mother that she looks as if she belongs in a fairy-story," the *Comte* said.

Susi knew he was thinking of the kiss that had awakened 'The Sleeping Beauty,' and she blushed.

"Why are we not staying in the Castle?" Trina asked.

"For two reasons," the *Comte* answered. "First because my grandmother who lives in the Dower House will chaperon you both, and secondly, for a reason I have not yet told your mother."

"What is it?" Susi asked a little apprehensively.

"I have let the Castle!"

"Let the—Castle?"

Susi repeated the words in a tone of sheer astonishment.

"Only for the summer months, but the sum I was offered was too good to refuse."

The *Comte* paused before he said:

"It will mean I can live there all through the winter without worrying about the expense."

Susi knew this explanation had a special meaning for her, but she said a little incoherently:

"But you—must not do—such a thing. I am—sure it will upset you and be horrible for you to think of having—tenants in the place you love so much."

"When the suggestion was made to me," the *Comte* said, "it seemed as if once again fate had taken a hand in my life and it was something I could not refuse."

Susi knew what he meant, but she could not look at him and it was left to Trina to ask:

"Who are your tenants? Are they very rich?"

"Immensely so," the *Comte* replied. "And they are English."

"English?"

"I do not know if you have ever heard of them," the *Comte* said, addressing Susi. "The Dowager Marchioness of Clevedon was, I believe, a very great beauty about ten or fifteen years ago."

"Of course I have heard of her," Susi answered. "I remember my father saying she was the loveliest woman he had ever seen in his life, and there were pictures of her in all the illustrated papers for years."

"That is what I understood," the *Comte* said. "Well, she wishes to rent Castle Girone because she believes by coming to Provence she will be able to regain her beauty."

Both Susi and Trina looked at him in astonishment.

"How can she do that?"

The *Comte* shrugged his shoulders.

"Provence has a reputation not only for restoring sick people to good health and having magic cures for almost every sort of disease, but most especially for retarding old age and restoring lost youth."

"Can that be true?" Susi asked.

"It is certainly one of the legends that is repeated and re-repeated especially around Arles."

"Why especially there?"

"The women in Arles," the *Comte* replied, "have a reputation, on which they pride themselves, of being the handsomest women in France. They attribute it to all sorts of herbs and potions of which apparently the Marchioness has heard rumours as far away as England."

"Do you believe in them?"

"To be quite truthful," the *Comte* replied, "I think their beauty comes from their combination of Roman blood mingled with Greek."

He smiled as he said:

"It is very obvious in their straight brows and beautifully chiselled noses, in their black eyes and hair which forms a dark misty halo round their rather haughty, often noble faces."

"I shall look forward to seeing them," Trina said.

"To make quite certain you notice them, they walk like Queens," the *Comte* smiled, "and they certainly do appear to remain looking young longer than women in other parts of the country."

"And are you also providing your tenants with the requisite ingredients?" Trina enquired.

"Actually when I saw the Marchioness two days ago, it was the one thing she wanted to talk about."

"I suppose everybody who is beautiful minds growing old," Susi said in her soft voice.

She was looking at Trina as she spoke, thinking it must be impossible for the *Comte* not to realise how lovely she looked as she listened to him attentively, her blue eyes raised to his.

"What I have promised to do," the *Comte* said ruefully, "is to find the Elixirs of Youth which have been written about in ancient books and manuscripts and which are somewhere in the Library of the Castle."

"I will help you find them," Trina offered, "and Mama, who can read French as easily as she reads English, will be another able assistant."

"We ought to find something between us to make the Marchioness feel that her money has not been wasted," the *Comte* laughed.

"Is she going to stay alone in the Castle?" Susi asked.

"No, I believe her son is coming with her for at least part of the time, and she talked about having a few guests to stay. I think as a matter of fact, she is intent only on keeping away the dreaded hands of Old Age."

"Perhaps that is what I shall be trying to do in a few years," Susi said in a low voice.

"Considering at the moment you look as young as Trina," the *Comte* said, "it will be at least another thirty years before you need begin to worry about your wrinkles and lines, and by that time I shall doubtless look like an octogenarian."

"Supposing we really find the Elixir of Youth," Trina said, following her own thoughts, "perhaps we could bottle it and sell it for enormous sums all over the world. The mothers of the girls who were at the Convent with me spent astronomical sums on creams and lotions to make themselves look beautiful."

"It is certainly an idea," the *Comte* remarked.

"We should make it compulsory, if they wish to buy it, to spend a month at an enormous rent, at the Castle," Trina went on, "and you would soon be so rich that you would never have to take another tenant."

"You are so full of ideas," the *Comte* said, "that I am going to insist that you and your mother

51

concoct this Elixir of Youth for the Marchioness. I must say when she asked me to procure it for her, I thought she was rather a bore and only agreed because I wanted her money. Now I find the idea rather entertaining."

"But of course, it is," Trina said, "especially if you have the right prescription hidden away in some musty old manuscript which nobody has looked at for years. Think of it, Mama, we can distil the herbs and mix them together!"

"We had better try it on ourselves first," Susi said, "to make certain our patient does not fall dead through some obscure poison!"

The *Comte* was smiling as he said:

"We must obviously go into partnership, but of course it will have to be a family business."

He looked at Susi as he spoke, but she was thinking how much more helpful Trina could be to him than she was.

She had young ideas, the enthusiasm of youth and the kind of vitality of which she thought the *Comte* should have in a wife.

'I am too old to make any enterprise a success,' she thought.

She wondered as she looked out of the window, why the sun did not seem to be shining as brightly as it had done before.

When they reached Arles there were two carriages waiting for them, the first a very impressive open carriage drawn by four well-bred horses, the other a Landau to carry the luggage and the servants.

"This is exciting!" Trina exclaimed as they set off. "I keep remembering that Provence is said to be one of the most beautiful parts of France."

"I think so," the *Comte* said simply and looking at Susi he added:

"It is a land for lovers because everywhere you will hear the nightingales."

Susi looked surprised and he went on:

"You will hear them before you go to sleep, singing to you of the love and romance which, to those who live here, is part of the very air they breathe."

He spoke in a deep voice which always gave Susi strange sensations which she found difficult to hide.

Because she felt shy she said quickly:

"I am glad there are nightingales. I have always been told that there are not so many small birds in France as in England because they are shot."

"You will find plenty of birds in Provence," the *Comte* replied. "On my own land the hills are alive with hares and boars, and there are also thousands of partridges and ortolan."

"We must not forget," Trina said, "that we have to concentrate on the herbs."

"I will show you where you can find plenty of those," the *Comte* smiled, "but I want you now particularly to notice that the air of Provence is scented with the fragrance of rosemary, lavender, thyme and orange blossom."

"I can see the spires of enough churches to

supply the bells for the latter," Trina said.

"Of course," the *Comte* agreed, and once again he was looking meaningfully at Susi.

They drove on and now both Susi and Trina began to grow excited as they had their first glimpse of the rock formation which they knew was characteristic of Provence.

White, glistening like sugar, it made everything look strange and pagan, at the same time, wildly romantic.

On some of the bare rocks rising high against the sky-line, there were the ruins of impregnable citadels which had never fallen to an enemy, while below them were eerie gorges that might have been the haunts of demons and supernatural beings.

It was all fascinating until suddenly the *Comte* bent forward to say:

"There is the Castle!"

It stood high above a silver river with the bare rocks rising behind it and its towers peaking towards the blue sky.

It looked strong and as if the centuries had made little mark upon it, and yet it had a beauty that made it part of the landscape, part of the mystery of the country itself.

"It is beautiful," Trina cried.

Susi knew the *Comte* was waiting for her to say what she thought, but for the moment she could only stare at the great building ahead of them.

Then because she knew that she must tell him what she felt, she said in a voice hardly above a whisper:

"It is exactly the—background you should—have and what—you must—keep."

He smiled as if he knew what she was thinking, and she knew too that he was pleased because his instinct told him that it meant something to her, as it did to him.

They crossed the river over an ancient bridge, then they were driving between trees, nearer and nearer to the Castle.

Trina was leaning out of the side of the carriage to see it more easily and the *Comte* put his hand over Susi's to say very softly so that only she could hear:

"Welcome to our home, my darling!"

She tried to look at him with an expression of warning in her eyes in case Trina should hear him, but all she managed was an expression of so much love that he felt almost as if she kissed him.

Then they passed the Castle and drove on to where perhaps less than a quarter-of-a-mile away behind some formal gardens was a Château built in the 18th Century.

The exquisite architecture which had been fashionable at the time was traditional of so many lovely French buildings of the period.

As the carriage drew up at the front door and the servants hurried down the steps to greet them, several small dogs came tumbling down too, to jump up at the *Comte* yelping with excitement.

There were some elderly servants whom he introduced to Susi and Trina, and then they walked through an exquisitely proportioned Hall

55

into a Salon which overlooked a flower-filled garden and beyond it the river.

In a chair was a woman who might have sat for a picture by Fragonard. Her hair beautifully arranged on top of her head was dead white, and although her face was old and lined it still held traces of the aristocratic beauty she had once possessed.

Her hands laden with rings were blue-veined as she held them out in welcome and there was no mistaking that she was delighted to see her grandson.

He kissed her hands, then both her cheeks.

"How are you, dearest boy?" she asked, speaking in English because their guests were English and it was only polite to speak their language rather than her own.

"I am happy to see you, *Grand'mère*," the *Comte* replied, "and now I wish to introduce my friends: First Lady Sherington, whom I am very anxious for you to meet, then her daughter Trina."

The *Comtesse* held out her hand, then said:

"Are my eyes deceiving me or perhaps in old age I have developed double vision."

The *Comte* laughed.

"It is extraordinary, is it not, *Grand'mère*, not one beautiful woman, but two exactly similar!"

"*C'est extraordinaire!*" the *Comtesse* agreed. "And now let me offer you some refreshment. You must be fatigued after such a long journey."

The servants brought them wine and delicious little pâtisseries that Trina found irresistible.

Then because there was still an hour before they must change for dinner, both Susi and Trina insisted they must see the Castle.

"How can we wait after all you have told us?" Trina said to the *Comte*. "Please, let us go there at once! Otherwise I am sure you will find me walking towards it in my sleep."

"Come along then," he said good-humouredly. "You know there is nothing I want more than to show the Castle to you both."

He included Trina in what he said, but he looked at Susi and she tried to tell herself he was only being polite and kind to her.

The Castle was, in fact, fantastic and Susi realised how much money had been spent in making its ancient walls the perfect background for the magnificent tapestries, pictures and furniture which had been collected down the ages.

There were Persian carpets that had been woven hundreds of years previously. There were gold-framed mirrors designed by the great masters of art, there were carved and gilded tables which matched them.

There were huge mediaeval fireplaces in which the trunk of a tree could smoulder every day and many carved in marble by craftsmen who were as great in their own way as the master painters who had decorated the ceilings with goddesses and cupids.

In every room they went Susi and Trina enthused until they had run out of admiring adjectives. Then they reached the Library.

There were thousands of books, most of them

bound in coloured leather tooled in gold and they stretched from floor to ceiling.

Trina looked around almost with an expression of despair.

"Have you any idea," she asked the *Comte*, "where the books on herbs we are seeking are likely to be?"

"Not at the moment," he replied, "but there is an old Librarian who comes twice a week to keep everything in order, and I am sure he will be able to tell us what we want to know."

"Thank goodness!" Trina replied. "Otherwise poor Mama and I will have to stay here for a hundred years to find what we require."

"That is what I want you to do," the *Comte* said.

Then with a change of mood, he said lightly:

"Look out of the window, there is something I want you to see."

They obeyed him, seeing only another magnificent view of the surrounding country.

"What particularly do you want us to look at?" Susi asked.

She turned as she spoke to find the room was empty.

"Jean!"

The door through which they had entered was still closed and there was no sign of him in the Library.

"Jean!" she cried again, feeling suddenly afraid because he had left her.

Then a portion of the bookcase flew open and there he was!

Trina gave a shriek of delight.

"That is one of the secret hiding-places! Oh, show me how to disappear, please, show me!"

The *Comte* explained to her that there was a little catch concealed in the ornamentation on the bookcase. He pressed it and the whole panel flew open.

Trina insisted on doing it for herself and as the bookcase shut behind her the *Comte* turned to Susi.

"Well, my precious?" he asked. "Will you be happy to live here with me?"

"You are—not to ask me that—question," Susi said quickly. "You know it is—something to which I must not—give you an—answer."

"I have already had my answer," the *Comte* retorted. "You told me you loved me and that was all I wanted to hear. This is to be our home, my lovely darling, and we will bring up our sons to love it and be as happy as we are."

"Oh—please—please—you must be—sensible," Susi pleaded.

He bent forward and just for one moment his lips rested on hers.

"That is being sensible!" he said quietly as the door of the bookcase opened and Trina came back into the Library.

Chapter Three

"HERE IS something fascinating!" Trina exclaimed. "It says in very difficult old French that *Comte* Bernhard not only magicked himself away but his weapons, his treasures, and his women. I wonder how many he had!"

She looked up as she spoke, then exclaimed:

"Mama, you are not listening!"

"I am—sorry," Susi answered, "what were you saying, dearest?"

She had been thinking of the *Comte* and of the trouble and difficulties she was making in his life.

Last night after dinner, just as the *Comtesse* was thinking of retiring to bed, the *Comte* had said:

"I hope, *Grand'mère* you will not mind if I move in here tomorrow."

"Move here!" the *Comtesse* had exclaimed in surprise. "But why should you wish to do that? What is wrong with the Castle?"

"There is nothing wrong," the *Comte* replied. "I have not had time to tell you before, but I have let it for the next three months."

There was a moment's silence as the old lady looked at him incredulously. Then she said:

"Let it? What do you mean—you have let it?"

"My tenant is the Marchioness of Clevedon," the *Comte* replied. "She and her son are, I believe, of great importance in England and they are very rich. Quite frankly, *Grand'mère*, I need the money."

"Never have I heard anything so extraordinary!" the *Comtesse* replied.

Then she was so agitated that she could only express herself in her own language and lapsed into French.

"*C'est incroyable!* Unbelievable that the *Comte* de Girone should stoop to taking money for his personal possessions from strangers! We may not be rich, but we are at least proud!"

"It is no use being proud without money," her grandson replied quietly.

"Money, money! Is that all you think about?" the Dowager cried. "If that is what you need, the remedy is very easy without your resorting to lowering yourself to the position of a shopkeeper with goods to sell."

"I do not think there is anything particularly degrading in letting the Castle to someone who will appreciate its beauty, and would not do anything to spoil its contents," the *Comte* remarked mildly.

"You think like an imbecile!" the old lady flared. "I know you are slightly embarrassed financially at the moment, but you are aware that it is only a question of time before you can take a wife and one who has the same dowry or perhaps a greater one, than Marie-Thérèse."

Her blue-veined hands were shaking with the intensity of her feelings. Then as the *Comte* did not speak, she added:

"I had a letter from your cousin Josephine only this morning. She tells me that the *Duc* de Soisson has already intimated that he would be proud for one of his daughters to be associated with the de Girones."

"When I want to marry the *Duc* de Soisson's daughter I will say so," the *Comte* said coldly. "I am not a young boy, *Grand'mère*, to have my marriage arranged for me as it was when I was twenty. Now I will decide whom I marry and I wish for no interference, however well meant, from any of my relatives."

His grandmother pressed her lips together and rang a silver bell which stood beside her.

When the servant came in answer to the summons, she merely indicated with a gesture of her hand that she wished to be wheeled from the room.

Without saying a word, gazing stonily in front of her, she left leaving an awkward silence behind.

The *Comte* poured himself a glass of brandy and after a moment Susi said in a small, frightened voice:

"I am—sorry your Grandmother is—upset—but she is right—of course it is upsetting and degrading for you to—let the home of your ancestors."

The *Comte* smiled.

"I assure you they have done far worse things in their time."

"That is—not the—point . . ." Susi began hesitatingly.

"I see no reason to discuss it," the *Comte* said quietly. "The Marchioness is arriving tomorrow."

They talked of other things, but it was an uncomfortable evening and when Susi went to bed she could not sleep but lay tossing and turning in the darkness.

She knew that it was her fault that the *Comte* was not prepared to marry the *Duc* de Soisson's daughter or any other girl with a huge dowry which would keep up the Castle in the way his first wife had been able to do.

"I must go away—I must—leave him," she told herself as she had done before.

But she knew that he would prevent her from doing so, or if she insisted, would follow her to England or wherever else she and Trina went.

"I must talk to him about it tomorrow," she decided.

But when the morning came, there seemed no opportunity for an intimate conversation.

As the Marchioness was arriving late in the afternoon, Trina insisted that they explore the Castle once again and immediately after luncheon they collected all the books they needed from the Library and had them carried to the Château.

They had already discovered quite a number of manuscripts which spoke of the efficacy of the local herbs, but Trina kept saying they still had not enough.

"Whatever we prepare for the Marchioness, it must have a dramatic effect the moment she drinks it," she insisted.

"It may make her feel well," Susi said, "but I cannot believe we can hope any herbs to be potent enough to perform miracles on her face."

Trina, however, was optimistic. She had found a number of references to the *Vinaigre des Quatre Voleurs* which was a potion containing an elixir of youth.

This was an extract which had been used at one time as a safeguard against contagious diseases, but the septuagenarian Queen of Hungary, who married the King of Poland when he was a very young man, attributed her attraction for him entirely to the elixir.

"It certainly contained wild thyme, fennel, and

rosemary, which every writer says retard old age," Trina said. "But there may be other things as well, and I am determined to find them."

She had realised ever since breakfast-time that her mother was only giving her half her attention, and now when she had not listened to what she had to say about Count Bernhard, she looked across the table and realised that Susi was looking very tired.

There were blue shadows under her eyes, and Trina thought for the first time since she had arrived from the Convent that her mother looked her age.

"What is the matter, Mama?" she asked coaxingly. "You look exhausted."

"I did not—sleep well," Susi admitted.

"Was it the *Comtesse* who upset you?" Trina asked. "Of course she is old, and to her the only thing that matters is the pomp and glory of the *Comtes* de Girone. But she is not prepared for them to be human."

"She believes they have a—responsibility for what has been—handed down to them—through the ages," Susi said in a low voice, "and which has to be—handed on to future—generations."

"Now you are siding with her. If the *Comte* does not want to marry some stupid young girl just because she is rich, why should he?"

"It is his—duty."

"That is nonsense, and very old-fashioned," Trina retorted.

At the same time, she was aware that she had not convinced her mother, and she wondered what she could say to make Susi realise how fortunate she was to have anyone so attractive and charming as the *Comte* in love with her.

'Poor Mama,' she thought, 'she has had a miserable time all these years, looking after Papa when he was ill and so disagreeable. I want her to enjoy herself, I want her to be happy.'

At the same time, because Susi had said nothing to her about the *Comte*'s intentions, Trina hesitated to broach the subject first.

She was sure Susi believed 'her little daughter' was quite unaware that he was passionately in love with her or that anyone, unless they were blind and deaf, would not have noticed the love in his eyes.

"If Mama wants me to appear half-witted I will act as she wishes," Trina said to herself, "but sooner or later I must prevent her from throwing away her happiness."

As she realised that Susi did not want to talk now she went on reading, quickly turning over the pages of a book.

Then the door opened and the *Comte* came in.

"She has—arrived?" Susi asked.

There was a note of anxiety in her voice, as if she felt something might have happened to disappoint him at the last moment.

"The Marchioness has arrived," he replied, "together with her retinue of lady's-maids, coachmen, her own special footman, and a secretary!"

Trina laughed.

"She certainly travels in luxury."

"You should see her luggage!" the *Comte* answered. "I thought when I first saw it that she must be intending to stay for three years rather than three months!"

"Perhaps the trunks are full of beauty-creams," Trina suggested.

"The moment I met her," the *Comte* said, "she started to talk of the youth-giving herbs she expects me to find for her. I only hope you have discovered something which will keep her happy, otherwise she intends to leave almost immediately."

"Leave?" Trina exclaimed.

The *Comte* sat down.

"It is hard to believe it," he said looking at Susi, "but I think the Marchioness is mad."

"Why should you think that?"

"She is utterly obsessed with this idea that somewhere in the world there is someone who will restore her beauty to what it was. She is nearly sixty and she expects some magician to make her look like Trina."

"Have you told her it is impossible?"

"I was trying to put some sense into her head," the *Comte* said, "and what do you think she said to me?"

"What?" Trina asked.

"That if the herbs and the magic of Provence cannot help her, then she intends to go immediately to Rome where Antonio di Casapellio has offered to perform the miracle she requires."

"Who is he and how can he do that?" Trina asked.

"By hypnotism."

Susi gave a little cry.

"But, surely that is dangerous?"

"Of course it is," the *Comte* replied, "I know all about Casapellio. He is a charlatan, a quack, and a crook!"

"Have you told the Marchioness so?"

"It would be useless if I did. She is convinced he can do what he says. She told me she is prepared to pay £10,000 to the man who will give her the Elixir of Youth!"

There was silence for a moment. Then Trina said:

"Did you say 10,000 pounds or francs?"

"Pounds," the *Comte* answered. "We were talking in English."

"It is unbelievable!" Susi exclaimed. "That is an enormous sum of money!"

"Yes, I know," the *Comte* agreed, "and I doubt if however hard you and Trina research you will find an elixir worth that sum."

There was another silence, then Trina asked:

"Is she prepared to pay *before* she tries it?"

"She is so stupid," the *Comte* said scornfully, "that she would pay anything to anyone who told her enough lies, which is exactly what Casapellio will do!"

"By hypnotising her into believing him?"

"The man is actually dangerous," the *Comte* replied, "but I do not see what I have to gain by maligning him. Besides, I am quite certain she will not believe a word I say against him."

"If she is so stupid she deserves everything she gets!" Trina said.

"It is not only that," the *Comte* said, in a worried tone.

"What else?" Susi enquired.

"A certain woman who went to Casapellio," the *Comte* replied, "and who was as rich as the Marchioness, was not only hypnotised by him, but he also doped her. He kept her in a twilight world under drugs and she died only after he had extracted from her every penny she possessed."

Susi gave a little cry of horror and Trina said:

"You must tell her the truth! However stupid she may be, she must realise what dangers she will encounter from such a charlatan."

The *Comte* did not reply and after a moment Susi said in a soft voice:

"You must—make her believe you."

She thought as she spoke that she herself could be persuaded by the *Comte* to believe anything he wished, and as if he knew what she was thinking, he smiled a little mockingly and said:

"You had better come and see her for yourself. You will then know that the Marchioness is a typical example of a pretty face that has nothing behind it."

"I would like to—convince—her."

"When she sees you, all she will want is to

look exactly like you," the *Comte* said.

There was a caressing note in his voice which sent a little quiver through Susi and which made Trina smile secretly to herself.

Because she was tactful she looked down at the book she had been reading and saw the reference to *Comte* Bernhard.

She gave a sudden scream which made both the *Comte* and Susi look at her in astonishment.

"I have an idea!" she cried. "I have a wonderful idea!"

"What is it?" Susi asked.

"Wait a minute, I have to think it out," Trina replied.

They waited and after a moment she said:

"It came to me when the *Comte* said the Marchioness would want to look like you, Mama. You will remember—or rather you will not, because you were not listening—what I told you about *Comte* Bernhard. Let me read it again."

Trina picked up the book and read slowly from the ancient French with its strange spelling:

"Monsieur le Comte with his wizardry and powerful sense of magic could not only disappear himself without sound or trace, but contrived by powers beyond mortal men to hide his weapons, his treasures and his women from the eyes of those who sought them."

Trina's voice seemed to vibrate round the Salon. Then as she finished speaking she looked at

71

her mother and the *Comte* and realised they did not understand what she was trying to say.

"You are being very slow," she said to the *Comte*, "I am trying to get you £10,000 and surely you see how easy it would be to make the Marchioness hand it over to you rather than to the Italian quack."

"I am trying to follow your line of reasoning," the *Comte* said, "but I do not see . . ."

"It is quite simple," Trina interrupted, as if she was impatient to give him time to think it out.

"You introduce Mama to her and first you tell the Marchioness how old she is. If she doubts your word she can look it up in Debrett. Then when Mama has drunk the Elixir, she will immediately look even younger because in her place there will be . . . me!"

Trina saw by the sudden glint in the *Comte*'s eye that he understood what she was trying to explain, but before he could speak Susi cried:

"But that would be deception—it would be— wrong!"

"It would be much more wrong," Trina objected, "for us to let this wretched woman go to Italy, to be doped by the Italian crook until she dies. Be sensible, Mama! We shall not only be doing her a favour, but we shall be collecting £10,000 for the *Comte*, to keep the Castle going for quite a long time."

"It is certainly an idea," the *Comte* said slowly. "But Susi is right. It is a deception."

"What does that matter?" Trina asked angrily. "Surely this is a case of the end justifying the means, as the Jesuits have preached for years?"

The *Comte's* eyes twinkled.

"You are beginning to persuade me."

"All I can say," Trina said, "is that you will be extremely stupid if you allow the £10,000 to slip through your hands."

She glanced at her mother as she spoke and saw that Susi was looking worried.

"It may seem shocking to you, Mama," she said, "and I know how you hate lies and deceit. But what is the alternative? Suppose we cannot dissuade the Marchioness from trusting this Italian and she dies under his treatment. Are you prepared to have that on your conscience?"

"Surely you can make her see sense?" Susi said to the *Comte*.

"Quite honestly I doubt it," he said. "When women are obsessed by one idea and can think of nothing else, all the wisdom of Solomon, combined with the eloquence of Demosthenes would not move them in another direction."

"But supposing," Susi said hesitatingly, "she— gives you the £10,000—and finds the Elixir is no good—she will still go to Rome after all."

The *Comte* made a gesture with his hands.

"That is a chance we have to take. At the same time, rich though she is, I cannot believe the Marchioness will be able to find another £10,000 so quickly. Perhaps she will wait a year and in that time grow not only older, but a little wiser."

Trina clapped her hands.

"I know you have accepted my idea," she said, "and now we must plan it very carefully. You must tell the Marchioness that you are not only procuring the Elixir of Youth for her, but in a day or two, you will be prepared to give her a demonstration of how it works."

She smiled before she added:

"The only difficulty is going to be that Mama does not look old enough, except perhaps today. She has lines under her eyes I have never seen before."

As if the *Comte* noticed them for the first time, he turned quickly towards Susi, putting out his hand towards her.

"What have you been doing to yourself?" he asked. "What has upset you?"

Trina got up from the table to walk to the far window as if she wanted more light to read the book she had in her hands.

"I am all—right," Susi replied.

Then as if she could not help herself, she put her hand in the *Comte's*.

His fingers tightened on hers.

"I know why you are worrying, my precious darling," he said in a low voice that only she could hear, "but leave everything to me, and of course, to your very intelligent daughter."

"We—should—go away."

"If you do, I shall come with you and I can promise you there is no place in Heaven or on earth where you can hide from me."

She raised her eyes, dark with worry to his, and he said very softly:

"I worship and adore you! If it meant I had to pull the Castle down brick by brick, I would not lose you now."

He spoke with so much sincerity that Susi felt the tears come into her eyes.

"How can you—say such—wonderful things to me?" she asked with a little sob in her voice.

"I will answer that question when we are alone," the *Comte* promised.

He raised her hand to his lips. As he kissed it, he saw a sudden radiance that seemed to transform her face and said very softly:

"I feel the same, and that is something neither of us can fight."

Trina came back to the table.

"I think we have enough material now to make the Elixir," she said in a practical tone. "It will be full of herbs which all through the ages, if your books are to be believed, have special properties, if not for actually rejuvenating the body, then at least, making it strong and well."

"I expect you have found the book written by Abbe Tisserand nearly thirty years ago. He came to Provence to die, but because of the air and our herbs, he lived to a remarkable old age," the *Comte* remarked.

"There are much older books than that," Trina said, "and every one of them says that rosemary has a rejuvenating effect on anyone who takes it."

"Here that is the easiest herb in the world to obtain," the *Comte* replied.

"We shall want thyme and basil," Trina said. "I will make a full list and the moment we have all the herbs Mama and I will begin distilling and mixing them until I am sure we shall begin to believe in the Elixir of Youth, as well as the Marchioness."

"Then—what do you—intend to do?" Susi asked nervously.

"That is where you have to play your part, Mama," Trina said firmly. "When you meet the Marchioness, talk to her and establish in her mind that you too are interested in being again as young as you once were."

"I shall be too—frightened to say anything," Susi said quickly.

"I shall be with you," the *Comte* remarked quietly.

"All you have to do is be yourself," Trina said. "Then when the *Comte* says he can obtain the Elixir of Youth from some Provencal witch who lives in a gorge or a cave in the rocks, you offer to take it and see what effect it has on you."

Trina looked at the *Comte*.

"You must make up your mind which room in the Castle we should use for this experiment."

"We have a considerable choice."

"Yes, of course," Trina agreed, "but I think the most dramatic one would be where the chair slides down through the floor."

"Perhaps you are right," he agreed. "The only

trouble is that however carefully we oil the machinery, the Marchioness might hear the slight noise that it makes."

"Unless I am mistaken, there is a piano in that room."

"Trina, you are a genius!" the *Comte* exclaimed. "I will say that the patient, who is Susi, must be in the dark while the Elixir works. We can surround her with screens or curtains, whichever is the most convenient. Then while I play, she sinks through to the floor below, and you take her place."

"That is exactly what we will do!" Trina cried. "And if you ask me, the whole thing will be a brilliant performance!"

"Supposing I—let you—down?" Susi faltered.

Once again the *Comte* took her hand in his.

"Leave everything to me," he said. "All you have to do is to look beautiful, and not quite as young as your daughter."

"I think we should make Mama when she meets the Marchioness," Trina said, "look a little older than she usually does."

"That will be difficult," the *Comte* replied.

"Not really," Trina answered. "Today with those shadows under her eyes she looks older, but tomorrow they may be gone unless we make certain they stay."

"What—do you—mean?" Susi asked apprehensively.

"I have my paint-box and crayons with me. You forget I have studied painting and drawing amongst other things at the Convent."

"And apparently Drama as well!" the *Comte* smiled.

"As it happens," Trina said, "I have read a lot of plays and I often think that were I a man I would like to be a producer."

"And not be an actress?" the *Comte* enquired.

Trina laughed.

"Can you imagine Mama's face if I suggested going on the stage?"

"I was only thinking of it in an amateurish capacity," the *Comte* replied. "I had one ancestor who had his own Theatre, not here, but in Paris. Of course he was emulating King Louis XIV because Madame de Pompadour produced the most amusing Comedies for him at the Theatre in Versailles."

"Now you are giving me ideas of what I can do in the future," Trina said.

Susi gave a little cry of protest.

"Do not encourage her!" she begged the *Comte*. "Can you imagine how shocked all our relations, especially my late husband's sisters will be, if Trina goes back to England with such ideas? As it is, they are certain that everything in France is the invention of the Devil!"

"Forget England and your relatives for the moment," the *Comte* said. "This is going to be amusing, Susi, and I promise you that although it may seem reprehensible, as far as the Marchioness is concerned, it is the better of two evils."

Trina laughed.

"Think that over, Mama, and know that you are really doing that stupid woman a good turn and saving her from herself."

"I do not—really know—what to—think," Susi faltered.

She looked at the *Comte* and added:

"But—if it will help you, I will do—anything you ask of me."

The expression in his eyes made her blush and Trina said:

"Let us get to work. The sooner we have that £10,000 in our hands the better!"

That night they dined alone because the *Comtesse* had not been seen all day.

When Susi enquired after her anxiously, the *Comte* replied:

"She is punishing us. All her life when *Grand'mère* is upset, she retires to bed to make those who have offended her feel guilty."

"What a funny idea!" Trina exclaimed.

"She realised it upset my grandfather when she was not there. He adored her because, as you can imagine, she was exceedingly beautiful, and although their marriage was arranged, they fell in love with each other the moment they met."

"Do tell me about your grandparents," Trina begged.

"*Grand'père* was extremely handsome and had been a roué until he married. But he and *Grand'mère* settled down at the Castle and I remember when I was a very small child realising how happy they were together."

The *Comte* smiled as he went on:

"But *Grand'mère*, despite her soft and feminine appearance, was a very determined person and she always got her own way. When *Grand-père* opposed her, she used to go to her bedroom and lock herself in. My father used to tell me how *Grand-père* would knock and knock without receiving an answer, until he apologised abjectly for something he had done."

The *Comte* laughed and went on:

"Then they would make it up and look radiantly happy in a way that made their love for each other very noticeable to everyone who saw them."

"No wonder you—wanted to be happy in the—same way," Susi said in a low voice.

Then she blushed as the *Comte* said quietly:
"I am!"

Trina walked out through the open window into the garden.

She knew from the way they were looking at each other that they would barely notice she had gone, except for being aware that they could now say things they prevented themselves from saying in her presence.

"I am sure the *Comte* wants to marry Mama, but she is being difficult about it," she reasoned.

"If he has the £10,000 it will help them to live fairly comfortably until I come into my father's fortune when I am twenty-one. Then I can give Mama what she should have had if Papa had not made that horrible and unfair Will."

It was impossible for Trina to give her mother anything at the moment, for her father had appointed Trustees who had complete control of her fortune until she came of age.

She had every intention then of giving her mother everything to which she believed she was entitled, but she knew it would be a mistake to say so now, in case they took steps, she was not certain how, to hinder her from circumventing her father's Will.

"I will keep quiet until it is too late for them to do anything or interfere in any way," she had told herself as soon as she heard what the Will laid down.

Now, however, she thought that if she told Susi exactly what she intended to do, then perhaps she would agree to marry the *Comte*, and they could all be very happy.

At the same time, she was astute enough to realise that he was humiliated by the knowledge that the money that had been expended on the Castle had come from the wife he had not loved and with whom he had been extremely unhappy.

Trina was as perceptive in her way as Susi was.

She noticed as they went round the Castle how every time they admired some new acquisition, a piece of tapestry, a fine oil-painting or some newly decorated room, there would be a defensive note in the *Comte*'s voice when he had to say: "My wife bought that," or "That was a gift from my late father-in-law."

"Because he has spent years being beholden to a woman," Trina reasoned, "it is obvious why he has no wish to be in the same position again."

But it was undeniable that the Castle cost an enormous amount of money to keep up, as well as the grounds with their beautiful gardens descending from flower-filled terraces to the river.

"Somehow I must find a solution," Trina told herself.

She had been walking all the time she was thinking out the problem, and now she found herself among the cypress trees which stood high above the river pointing like fingers towards the darkening sky.

The sun had sunk but there was still a faint glow far away on the horizon, the first stars were coming out overhead and a half-moon was throwing its beams down onto the moving water.

It was very lovely, at the same time it had a strange, almost unreal mystery about it that she could not remember having experienced before.

It was almost as if the stories of the magic and enchantment of Provence being different from anywhere else in France, were true. Even as she thought of it she heard the nightingales.

They were not very near, and yet in the silence of the deepening dusk they seemed first to attract her attention, then to come nearer and still nearer so that she listened entranced to the music made by what she knew were two birds.

One sang to the other and would then wait for the reply, after which they sang in unison and Trina felt as if her heart sang with them.

She heard a quiet step behind her and she thought the *Comte* had come in search of her, and held up her hand so that he should not speak or break the spell.

The nightingales trilled on, until still singing their voices grew fainter and Trina knew they were flying up towards the stars.

She felt almost as if she could see them and follow them, but as she threw back her head to search the sky, she could see only the glitter of the stars and the light from the moon.

For a moment she felt as if she too could fly. Then remembering that the *Comte* was beside her, she gave a little sigh and came back to reality.

"That was a song of love," she said softly and turned her head.

To her astonishment, it was not the *Comte* who stood there, but a man she had never seen before.

He was very tall and broad-shouldered, and it was light enough for her to see he was handsome, but in a very different way from the *Comte*, in fact in a manner that was peculiarly English.

For a moment they stared at each other as the light from the moon haloed Trina's fair hair. Then as the man beside her did not speak, she said:

"I think you must be the Marquis of Cleve-don."

He smiled.

"And I am sure you are Lady Sherington. The *Comte* told me you were staying here."

Trina was just about to say that she was in fact, Lady Sherington's daughter when she remembered that it was important that the Marchioness should not know of her existence.

Just in time she replied:

"That is clever of you."

"Not really," the Marquis replied. "Our host told my mother what a very lovely guest he had staying with him, and may I tell you he did not exaggerate?"

"Thank you."

Trina did not blush or feel embarrassed by the compliment because unlike Susi, she had received so many when she was in Rome.

She looked away from the Marquis down at the river and towards the distant, darkening horizon.

"So you were listening to the song of love," the Marquis said. "I was not told that nightingales were a part of the attractions of Provence."

He spoke with a slightly mocking note in his voice which told Trina without words that he was rather dubious about what he had heard of this part of France, and that doubtless included the Elixir of Youth which his mother was seeking.

As he spoke she was thinking with surprise that the *Comte* had not mentioned his arrival at the same time as the Marchioness.

"When I was driving here this evening from where I have been staying," he said, almost in answer to her unspoken question, "I thought how beautiful and unusual the countryside was. I have not visited this part of France before."

"Neither have I, and I find it very exciting."

"I should have thought 'romantic' was a better word," the Marquis remarked. "When I saw you silhouetted against the cypress trees I thought you must be a nymph from the river, or perhaps a ghost from the past."

"You are certainly entering into the spirit of the place," Trina said, "and surely you find the Castle different from any building you have ever seen before."

"It is certainly very magnificent."

Again there was that slightly mocking note in his voice, as if he was determined to be cynical about everything, and perhaps everybody.

"I think perhaps I should return to the Château," Trina remarked.

"Must you leave me alone with my thoughts?" the Marquis asked.

"Are you afraid of them?"

"Not in the least, but I would rather you stayed with me."

"I am of course honoured," Trina said, "but I have a feeling that your anxiety for my company is because it is me or no-one!"

The Marquis laughed.

"Perhaps I am not as eloquent as a Frenchman

would be in the circumstances, but shall I say in plain English that I would like to talk to you. Why do we not sit down?"

He indicated as he spoke, a stone seat which Trina had not noticed before, placed a little to the side of them and protected at the back by two tall cypress trees.

Without arguing Trina moved towards it, aware that Susi and the *Comte* would not be anxious for her to rejoin them and if she was honest she was rather interested in the Marquis.

She had a feeling that it would be a mistake to under-estimate his intelligence and, however foolish and gullible his mother might be, he would be very different.

Trina seated herself on the stone seat and the frills of her bustle swept the ground very elegantly beside her. Her waist silhouetted against the cypress trees looked very tiny, while her bare neck and shoulders glowed white in the light from the moon.

The Marquis sat beside her and turned so that he was almost facing her.

Trina knew that his eyes were on her face and she wondered what he was thinking.

"I still feel," he said after a moment, "that you are not real. The Castle, the moonlight, the nightingales are a fantasy, and even if I find them here in the morning, you will have disappeared."

"I hope I shall sleep most of the night comfortably in my bed."

"Now I know that you are English," the Marquis remarked. "Only an Englishwoman would sweep away the poetry of the moment with such a practical remark!"

"Only an Englishman would be uncouth enough to point out to her where she had failed him!" Trina flashed.

The Marquis laughed and answered:

"I have been staying in a French household, and I am trying to emulate the ease with which a Frenchman can pay compliments. But I know now it is the result of a lifetime of endeavour and practice."

"While a Frenchman is learning the art," Trina said, "an Englishman is studying how to bowl a cricket-ball, or how to punch another boy on the nose!"

"I have an uncomfortable feeling that is true, because I remember going through a phase of disliking women, and wondering what possible use they could be in the world."

"A Frenchman knows the answer to that when he first opens his eyes!" Trina smiled.

"You do not believe everything a Frenchman says to you?" the Marquis asked.

"Of course I want to do so! It is just that some critical, very English part of my brain warns me I should not believe a word they say!"

The Marquis laughed again.

"I think we will agree and disagree on quite a number of subjects, one way or another," he said, "but I shall be hoping, and I say this with a very English sincerity, that you will not leave before I return."

"You are going away?"

"I only came tonight to see that my mother was safely installed in the Castle," he replied. "Tomorrow I go to Monte Carlo, but only for a week or so."

"Then I expect I shall be here, My Lord, when you return."

"That is exactly what I wanted to hear."

Trina rose to her feet.

"May I wish you *Bon Voyage* and *Bonne Chance* at the card-tables?"

"I have a feeling I shall find them very dull and prosaic after the magic of the nightingales and of course, you!"

"Now that is very flattering and very French!"

Trina held out her hand as she spoke and the Marquis took it in his.

"Good-night, Lady Sherington!"

He seemed to hesitate for a moment, then he bent his head.

As she felt his lips on her hand she had a feeling that it was not a perfunctory kiss of politeness and she told herself it was a very good thing he was going away.

Too late she thought that this had been the type of conversation in which Susi would never have taken part, and it would be difficult to explain to her exactly what had been said or how she must carry it on when the Marquis returned.

Quickly Trina took her hand from his and moving through the cypress trees she hurried over the lawns back towards the Château.

He made no move to follow her and she had the feeling that he thought perhaps it might embarrass her and also that he might be encroaching on the *Comte's* preserves.

"He is intelligent and perceptive," Trina told herself.

She thought that when the *Comte* had spoken of her mother he would not have been able to prevent the warmth in his voice and the expression in his eyes that Susi always evoked in him.

She also guessed that the Marquis, being convinced that she was Lady Sherington, a married woman and a widow, had flirted with her as he would not have attempted to do with a young girl.

He had a definite fascination of his own. He was very different from the *Comte* and yet in his own way he was extremely attractive.

Trina told herself regretfully that in other circumstances it would have been fun to meet him again and talk to him. In a strange way she could not quite determine, he made her feel provocative.

She had not met many Englishmen. There had been some in Rome, but she had spent most of the time with the older brothers and their friends of the Italian girl with whom she was at the Convent, and who had invited her to stay.

They had been prepared to flatter her from

first thing in the morning until last thing at night, but she had always kept them at arm's length, laughing at their eloquence and not taking anything they said seriously.

It had been an experience that had given her a sophistication she had not had before, even though her time in Spain had taught her a great deal about men and their approach to women.

Of all the men Trina had met the Marquis was different. Perhaps it was because he was English, or maybe because he was older. She guessed him to be twenty-nine or thirty.

Although she had no reason for thinking so, she had the feeling that he was slightly rakish, and perhaps as much a heart-breaker in his own way, as the *Comte* was in his.

Whatever he might be, as she reached the Château she told herself this was the last time she would be able to see him.

It was a dispiriting thought, and she wished it was not so imperative to play a trick on the Marchioness and extract £10,000 from her.

Chapter Four

WHEN TRINA got back to the Château she decided to go straight to bed.

As she passed the Salon she could hear the voices of her mother and the *Comte* and was certain they did not want to be interrupted.

When she was undressing it struck her again that it was really very strange that the *Comte* had not said the Marquis was at the Castle.

They had obviously met and talked together, and it would have been natural for him to mention his presence when he returned to the Château for dinner.

Then on thinking it over, she decided the reason he had not done so was that he was well aware that the Marquis with his cynical, slightly sceptical attitude towards everything, would frighten Susi.

'He is sensible in that,' Trina thought, 'because Mama is very easily frightened, and I am sure of one thing, she would never have been able to talk to the Marquis as I did tonight.'

It was extremely lucky that he was leaving tomorrow morning, and she decided that once they had the £10,000 they must all leave.

She had the uncomfortable feeling that however easy the Marchioness might be to deceive, it would be very hard to do the same where the Marquis was concerned.

Then she told herself she was being unnecessarily apprehensive.

Who would imagine in their wildest dreams that there would be two women, mother and daughter, who looked so much alike as she and Susi?

At the same time Trina was aware that, while there was a superficial likeness in that their hair, their skin and their eyes were the same colour, inevitably to any observer who was searching deeper and was suspicious, there were obvious differences.

Susi, despite her youthful appearance, had given birth to a child and in consequence her breasts were a little fuller than Trina's, her waist not quite so small.

Also the way she moved did not have the spontaneous buoyancy of a girl of eighteen, while her face had a slight sharpness about its outline, un-like the softness of Trina's.

Apart, it would be easy for them to impersonate each other, but if they stood together, Trina was astute enough to guess that someone like the Marquis would be able without hesitation, to pick out who was the elder of the two.

"We shall have to leave," she told herself again, but that did not mean they would have to return to England.

They could stay in Paris where the *Duchesse* would be only too pleased to act as hostess.

"It has been such a short visit, Susi dearest," she had said as they were leaving. "I quite understand that you want to see Jean's Castle, but when you are tired of country life, come back to Paris, and I will make you and Trina the most sought after young women in the whole city."

She was speaking sincerely and Trina had thought at the time that she would love to accept such a generous invitation.

'It would be very good for Mama to be a success,' she thought, thinking more of her mother than of herself. 'She has always been crushed and snubbed by those horrible old sisters of Papa, and when she was nursing him she never thought of doing anything of which he would not approve.'

As she got into bed, Trina thought once again of how she could help her mother financially once she was twenty-one.

"In the meantime," she decided, "I can pay for her clothes, pretending they are mine, and if the Trustees complain I am extravagant, I will make myself so objectionable that they will give me all the money I want."

She wanted to go on thinking about her mother, but somehow insidiously she found herself going over her conversation with the Marquis.

"I suppose, if I am honest, he is the most attractive man I have ever seen," she told herself before she fell asleep.

With the morning came the first difficulties of making sure that neither the Marchioness nor any member of her household was aware of Trina's existence.

"It means we cannot all ride together," the *Comte* said. "I am sorry, Trina, but when we made our plans, I did not realise how restricting this would be for you."

"I can put up with a good deal of discomfort as long as you get the £10,000," Trina smiled. "It would be best for you to take Mama riding while I begin work in the Still-room. When I peeped in before breakfast, I saw great bundles of rosemary."

"There is also thyme and fennel," the *Comte* said, "and I have told the gardeners to bring in a number of other herbs which grow in the Castle gardens and which I am sure you will find useful. There is comfrey for one, and French tarragon, which I am sure should be added to the Elixir."

"Of course they must!" Trina agreed, "and if the lilies-of-the-valley are not over, I would like to have a few of those as well."

"You may have anything you wish," the *Comte* said. "How long do you think it will take you to make this magic potion?"

"I want to do it quickly and get it over with," Trina replied. "You know until the drama has taken place Mama will worry! If we take too long she will actually look so old that the contrast between us will make the transformation seem very necessary!"

"You can leave your mother to me," the *Comte* said to Trina.

She had the feeling, although he had not said so, that he too was thinking that everything must be done and finished with before the Marquis returned.

She went to the Still-room which fortunately was not used by the *Comtesse*'s staff, and with the ancient manuscripts and books to guide her, she started to chop up the herbs.

She soaked the juices from them, mixed them with each other one by one, until she had achieved a fairly palatable flavour.

Herbs are never very appetising at the best of times, and Trina decided it would be wise to add honey to the potion to sweeten it.

Her Nanny had told her when she was a child,

95

that honey had special 'magical' qualities because the Queen Bee lived for twenty years, and there had always been a comb of fresh honey from the bees on her father's estate on the Nursery table.

At luncheon-time she asked the *Comte* if there was a special honey to be found in Provence.

"Of course there is," he said, "in fact, quite a number of them. There is thyme-honey, lavender-honey, and a very special one which the bees make from the spring flowers . . ."

"Which of course must go into our Elixir of Youth," Trina finished.

The *Comte* promised to order some to be brought to the Château. Then he said:

"This afternoon I am taking your mother to call on the Marchioness. I think, Trina, this is where you must apply the little touches of old age that she does not possess naturally."

Because she had been so happy on her ride with the *Comte*, Susi looked young and very lovely.

"I think really," Trina said jokingly, "it is I who should pretend to be Lady Sherington and Mama can come up in the chair as me!"

"It is certainly an idea," the *Comte* laughed, but Susi cried:

"You are both making me feel shy! If I do look young it is only because I am so happy."

"That is what I want you to be," the *Comte* said in his deep voice.

They looked into each other's eyes, and Trina was forgotten.

Later she went to her mother's bedroom where Susi was changing into an elegant afternoon-gown, one which made her look older than the comparatively simple white dresses did, which constituted the main part of her wardrobe.

It was another of the gowns she had worn when she was in mourning, of pale palma violet, the skirt having frill upon frill of pleated chiffon edged with lace, which was echoed on the bodice and on the sleeves.

There was a sash of mauve velvet around her waist, and Trina decided her mother must wear a necklace of amethysts with ear-rings and bracelet to match.

"I have always thought this set old-fashioned and stuffy," she said, "and I am quite certain Aunt Dorothy influenced Papa into buying it for you! But it is just what you want at the moment."

"He gave me so many beautiful jewels," Susi said, "that I would be very ungrateful if I complained."

"You never complained, Mama, but you know as well as I do the amethyst is a dull stone, but I love your diamonds and of course, the turquoises."

"You may wear anything I possess," Susi said.

"And that applies the other way around, Mama," Trina replied. "When you marry the *Comte* and no longer have a lot of money to spend on such frivolities as clothes, I intend to buy all your gowns for you and they will be a present from me to you."

"You must do nothing of the sort!" Susi said automatically.

Then she added quickly:

"What makes you—think I will—marry the *Comte*?"

"But of course you will marry him, Mama," Trina said. "He is so attractive, charming, and very much in love with you."

"How can I—allow him to—give up so—much for—me?" Susi asked in a low voice.

As she spoke Trina knew without her mother telling her so, that the *Comte* did want to marry her and had already said so.

"He has been very unhappy with one wife whom he married for money," Trina said in a practical tone. "You can hardly condemn him to spend the rest of his life being unhappy with another one."

"But suppose," Susi said in a very small voice, "after we are—married he—regrets that he—cannot spend so much money on the—Castle?"

"If you think like that, Mama," Trina said, "then I can only believe you are not really in love."

Susi looked at her in a startled fashion as she went on:

"I am sure the *Comte* loves you as he has never loved anyone before in his whole life, and although you are making difficulties, Mama, you are well aware that you love him in the same way."

Susi's eyes filled with tears.

"Oh, Trina—I am so worried—what am I to do?"

"Marry him, and let him do all the worrying!"

Trina put her arms round her mother as she spoke and kissed her cheek.

"How can you be so foolish?" she asked. "You have the most attractive man one could imagine madly in love with you, and offering you an exciting life away from England and all those disagreeable relatives of Papa's. Personally, I would not hesitate for a second to snap him up before somebody else does!"

"Oh, Trina—you do say such—terrible things!" Susi complained.

But her tears had turned to laughter.

"I am so lucky, so very, very lucky," she said, a sob still in her voice, "to have you and—Jean, and I have not known for years what it is like to laugh, to feel as if I could dance, or fly in the sky."

"That is love!" Trina said.

As she spoke she remembered how, last night, the nightingales had flown away towards the stars singing their song of love.

She made Susi wipe her eyes and very delicately she drew in a soft shadow underneath them and added what appeared to be several faint wrinkles at the corners.

She stood back to see the effect of what she had done.

"Look at me, Mama," she ordered and as Susi did so, said:

"I suppose it does make you look a little older, but you are still absolutely lovely. I am not surprised that the *Comte* was bowled over the first moment he saw you."

It flashed through her mind that the Marquis might have felt exactly the same about her.

Then she told herself that he was much more cynical than the *Comte* and it would take a great deal more than a pretty face to upset his well-established equilibrium.

Trying not to think about herself or the Marquis, Trina concentrated on arranging her mother's hair in a slightly different style, then placed on it a very elaborate bonnet of mauve flowers and velvet ribbons which matched the gown.

"You look as though you might be going to Ascot or a Reception at Marlborough House rather than making a simple afternoon call in the country," she smiled.

"Do you think Jean will—think I am—overdressed?" Susi enquired anxiously.

"It will not matter what the *Comte* thinks," Trina replied. "You have to concentrate, Mama, on the Marchioness. Do not forget to sympathise about her search for the Elixir of Youth and say it is something you have always wanted to find yourself."

Finally Susi was ready and, when they went downstairs together, Trina knew that the *Comte* was delighted with her efforts.

To make Susi feel at ease he talked to her in a way which brought the colour to her cheeks which were rather pale and made her eyes shine.

"He is just the sort of husband Mama should have," Trina told herself as she watched them drive away in the open carriage.

It was to take them the long way round so that they could arrive in style, entering the Castle by the drawbridge which spanned the moat, to drive into the court-yard in the centre of the building.

At the back of the Castle there were green lawns right up to the ancient walls and formal gardens laid out, the *Comte* had told Susi, in the reign of Louis XIV.

Trina however, wasted no time in watching them but ran upstairs to the Still-room.

When, over an hour later Susi and the *Comte* returned, a servant came to tell Trina that *Monsieur le Comte* and *Madame* were waiting for her in the Salon.

She pulled off the apron with which she had covered her gown while she was working, washed her hands and ran downstairs.

Susi had already taken off her bonnet and placed it beside her long kid gloves and her hand-bag on a chair.

"What happened? Tell me!" Trina exclaimed as she hurried across the room.

The *Comte* deliberately waited for Susi to speak first.

"The Marchioness must have been very beautiful," she said in her soft voice, "but, Trina, she is really rather pathetic."

"In what way?"

"She obviously cares for nothing and nobody except her lost looks! Oh, dearest, I hope I shall never be like that!"

"How could you be?" Trina asked. "You never think of yourself, but spend your time in worrying over other people."

"I can see the Marchioness is going to be added to the list," the *Comte* said, "but your mother is right—she is pathetic."

"She looked—quite wild," Susi said, "when she insisted she must find—the Elixir of Youth."

"Did you tell her there was one?" Trina asked.

"Jean—did that."

"What your mother is trying to tell you is that she is not a good liar," the *Comte* smiled. "I told the Marchioness that a wonderful age-old secret Elixir would be here in two days. Was that too soon?"

"No, I think I can have it ready by then," Trina replied, "but I wish we had taken a little time in rehearsing going up and down through the floor in the moving chair."

"I suppose we could use one of the other secret entrances," the *Comte* said, "but you are right in thinking it is far more convincing if somebody disappears from the centre of the room than if they sat near to a wall or a book-case which could be immediately suspect."

"We will manage," Trina said, "but I meant to ask you to find a very ancient-looking apothecary's bottle in which to put the Elixir, once it is ready."

"I know exactly what you want," the *Comte* replied.

"But for the moment, go on telling me what the Marchioness said," Trina begged.

"She is still beautiful in a somewhat faded manner," Susi answered, "but the dye she has used on her hair is rather bright and it gives her an unreal look, as if she was a painted doll."

"I know what you mean," Trina said. "Perhaps we could make her a different kind of dye. Some of the books give details about which herbs to use and how to dye the hair, including one which says that the blood of a hare is very efficacious in helping it to grow."

Susi looked shocked.

"I can think of nothing more unpleasant!"

"There are much worse prescriptions than that!" Trina said. "But you were telling me about the Marchioness. What did you talk about?"

Susi smiled.

"She talked, but only about her looks and how many different treatments she has tried. She went to Paris last year."

"I am sure they made her pay something horrifying for what she required," the *Comte* remarked.

"According to her they promised all sorts of improvements," Susi answered, "but when she went back to England she thought the massage they had given her on her face had made the skin loose."

"I should think that was quite likely to happen," Trina said.

"That was what made her decide," Susi went on, "that external treatments were useless and that somehow, somewhere, she would find the Elixir of Youth."

"Did she say again what she would pay for it?" Trina enquired.

"She actually said," Susi replied, "that she would give every penny she possessed if she could look as she did in the days when people stood on chairs in the Park to watch her pass and her carriage was mobbed when she attended the Opera or went to the Theatre."

"In a way I can understand what she feels now."

"It has made me determined to grow old gracefully," Susi said. "Please, if you ever see me fussing about my face, tell me I am being a fool and that there is nothing that can make time stand still."

She spoke to Trina, but she looked at the *Comte* and he said quietly:

"I think every age has its attractions. To me *Grand'mère* is still very lovely, and I admire her more every time I see her."

"Have you seen her today?" Trina asked.

The *Comte* nodded.

"She has forgiven me enough to grant me an

udience! At the same time, she intends to keep
o her own room until she feels she can face a
vorld in which her grandson would demean him-
elf for mere money!"

He spoke in a way which made Trina laugh at
vhat he said, but Susi remarked:

"If only you did not—have to—upset her."

"One thing she said firmly and in a manner in
vhich I know she means it," the *Comte* said,
"and that is that she will never meet my tenant."

He paused to add:

"It is the best thing that could happen. I was
wondering how we could tell *Grand'mère* on no
account to mention Trina's existence."

"Everything is working out for the best," Trina
said, "and that will be achieved when you receive
the sum of £10,000 and we can all leave."

"Do you think—that is what we—must do?"
Susi enquired.

"But of course," Trina said. "We do not want
to be here when the Marchioness finds the Elixir
does not work in the way she expects it to. But
I promise you one thing, she will certainly feel
better in health."

"She does not look well," Susi said. "I think,
although I may be mistaken, that she diets to
excess to keep her figure. She would not eat
anything at teatime, although she gave us a large
and delicious English tea."

"When you have time, Mama," Trina said, "I
want you to come and sample the Elixir I have
concocted so far. It tastes rather nice, but I want

to be quite certain it does not give you indiges
tion or make you feel dizzy."

"You are not to upset your mother," the *Comt*
said quickly. "Let me try the Elixir."

"Of course you can," Trina replied, "but
doubt if your reactions would be as sensitive a
Mama's."

"We will both try it," Susi said firmly.

She and the *Comte* each drank a wine-glassfu
before they went to change for dinner and whe
they came down to the Salon Susi said:

"I am trying to decide whether I feel any dif
ferent. I feel so well anyway that it is difficult t
know what effect the Elixir could have on me."

"What about you?" Trina enquired of the
Comte.

"I feel as if I could push the world over, swim
the Channel and fly to the moon!" he replied.

"It is not the Elixir that makes you feel like
that!"

"I know," he answered, "but your mother wil
not believe me when I tell her she is the only
Elixir I need!"

"Then make her believe you," Trina said and
they smiled at each other in a conspiratorial fashion.

They laughed a lot during dinner which was
a delicious meal, and when it was over Trina
thought that once again she should leave her
mother and the *Comte* alone.

Without their even noticing what she was
doing she walked out of the window as she had

done the night before and onto the lawn.

The moon was fuller and when she reached the place where she had heard the nightingales the moonbeams were already rippling on the river touching it with silver as it twisted away between the high banks.

She could not hear the nightingales, so she moved towards the stone seat where she had sat with the Marquis and wondered what he was doing.

Had he thought of her today as she had thought of him?

She was sure that in Monte Carlo he would find innumerable glamorous and sophisticated women who would be only too willing to flirt with him and make his stay there extremely entertaining.

She wondered why he was not married, and thought perhaps he was one of the fashionable men who she heard danced attendance on the much acclaimed social beauties and in the words of one cynic: "Spent their time going from Boudoir to Boudoir."

Trina knew, as it happened, quite a lot about London Society although there had been few English girls at the Convent.

When she had been first in Madrid and then in Rome, she had listened to the gossip which was the main topic of conversation amongst the grown-ups and found she learned not only about the amorous intrigues of the country she was in, but also about her own.

It was obvious that the Prince of Wales was not only greatly admired on the Continent, but that his love-affairs—there were a great number of them—were known and talked about from Bordeaux to Warsaw and from Madrid to the shores of the Adriatic.

Because she was curious she had written home to her mother to ask her to send her every week the *Illustrated London News*, the *Graphic*, and the *Ladies Journal*.

She found in them pictures of all the Society Celebrities she had heard about and studied them with interest.

It was a world in which Susi had taken a small part before her husband became ill and incapable of leaving his home.

Trina could remember when she was a little girl how lovely her mother had looked wearing a diamond tiara which was part of the Sherington collection, a diamond necklace which had always seemed to be too heavy for her neck, and the bracelets, rings and brooches which would really have suited a much older woman.

"You look like the Fairy Princess, Mama!" she had said. "Perhaps the Prince will be waiting for you at the Ball."

Susi had smiled.

"Papa is my Prince, dearest."

At the time Trina had thought that her Papa, distinguished though he appeared, was really too old to be the Prince in a fairy-story.

It struck her now that the sort of Prince she

had been envisaging for her mother would have looked very much like the Marquis.

As she thought of him, almost as if she had conjured him up out of her thoughts, someone sat down beside her on the stone seat.

She gave a little exclamation of sheer astonishment.

It was the Marquis, and with the moonlight on his face he seemed even more handsome, more broad-shouldered and more over-powering than he had the night before.

"Good-evening, Lady Sherington," he said. "It is obvious you are surprised to see me."

"I . . . thought you had . . . left for Monte Carlo," Trina replied, finding it somehow difficult to speak.

"I did," he answered, "but when I reached Arles I was told that the trains were late owing to a landslip of some sort, on the line. I waited for several hours, then decided I had no intention of staying in an uncomfortable Hotel and came back here for the night."

Trina gave a little sigh of relief.

This meant he had not seen her mother although for one perplexing moment, she had thought perhaps Susi and the *Comte* had entered into a conspiracy not to tell her that the Marquis was at the Castle.

"You will be leaving tomorrow?" she asked aloud.

"Are you in such a hurry to get rid of me?" he enquired.

"No, of course not! I was only interested. It must be upsetting for you to have your plans altered at the last moment."

"Shall I confess that I was glad to have the opportunity of seeing you again?"

"You can hardly expect me to believe that."

"Then shall we say I was feeling romantic and hoped that the nightingales were in good voice."

"Have you noticed that they have decided not to give a performance tonight?"

"How disobliging of them. I shall have to make do with you. Will you sing me a song of love?"

"I doubt my voice would be as beguiling."

"Then we must talk instead," the Marquis said. "And now that we know each other so much better, I suggest you tell me about yourself."

"That would be very dull," Trina replied. "As it happens, when you suddenly appeared I was thinking about you."

"You were thinking of me?" he asked quizzically.

Trina realised he was not likely to let such an opening pass and she replied:

"Not particularly personally, but of the social life in which I am sure you play a prominent role."

"I can tell by your tone of voice that it does not particularly impress you."

"I am not prepared to criticise, except that it is a world of which I know nothing except what I have read and heard."

"Which I am convinced, was not only inaccurate, but slanderous!"

Trina gave a little laugh.

"How can you be sure of that?"

"Tell me to whom you have listened on the subject. I am sure I can tell you exactly what they said."

"I think that would be very indiscreet," Trina retorted, "but you are well aware that Europe as a whole is fascinated by the Prince of Wales and those who are considered his friends."

"I understood from my mother," the Marquis said, "that this was your first visit to France."

Too late Trina realised she had for the moment forgotten she was supposed to be Susi for she had been thinking of her own visits to Madrid and to Rome.

"I stayed in Paris on my way here, My Lord."

She hoped, by improvising thus on the spur of the moment, she had covered up any slip she might have made.

"Then I expect you found the gossip of the Parisians very informative," the Marquis said.

"I found them very fascinating," Trina replied, hoping to change the subject.

"Actually we were talking about me," the Marquis reminded her, "and I was flattered when you admitted to thinking about me, as I have thought about you."

"Why?" Trina asked.

"Because you are not only different from what

I expected, but in a way, different from anybody I have ever met before."

"I am not going to ask in what way," Trina said defensively.

"Then I will tell you," the Marquis replied. "You are beautiful, as you are well aware, but there is something else: a kind of vibration that comes from you which I have never encountered before, but which I find definitely intriguing."

"Once again you are speaking in a very un-English manner."

If she wished to divert him from making too intimate observations about herself, she was unsuccessful.

"It may seem to you un-English," the Marquis replied, "but I suppose the majority of us consider only the words which we hear and seldom look deeper for the motives or feelings or truth which underline them."

What he said immediately intrigued Trina.

"I am sure you are right," she said in a very different voice from what she had used before. "Words are only a vehicle and often very inadequate to express emotions. That is why I believe all the great teachers of mankind used an esoteric language when they spoke to their pupils which so far has never been adequately interpreted by the uninitiated."

"Who told you that?" the Marquis asked.

"It does not matter . . . but it is true, is it not?"

"So you think that the disciples of whatever Messiah they were following, sensed what they were taught more than simply by hearing with their ears?"

"Of course," Trina replied. "That is exactly what I wanted to say to you, but you have expressed it better than I could."

"I think you express it very ably, by just being yourself."

Trina gave a little sigh.

"Now you are making everything personal again. I was enjoying talking to you because we were both using our brains and that I am sure is unusual."

She was thinking as she spoke, that this was just the type of conversation she had always wanted to have with somebody cleverer than herself.

The teachers at the Convent, even the best of them, had been unable to answer the questions which she had put to them and she had found only some of the answers she sought in the books which she read.

Many of these, however, were so erudite that the Mother Superior of the Convent had told her scornfully they were far beyond her comprehension.

But Trina had always wanted to seek the unattainable.

She thought now that the Marquis quite unexpectedly was somebody she had always sought not because he was an attractive man, but because he had obviously been thinking along the same lines as herself.

"I suppose," the Marquis said, as if he was reasoning it out for himself, "while nursing your husband during the years he was sick, you had nothing else to do but read."

Again Trina was startled to realise that she was supposed to be Susi.

"Yes . . . of course," she said quickly. "I had . . . plenty of time for that."

"Are you surprised I find you different?" the Marquis asked. "Most women who are as beautiful as you are, worry about their looks, seldom about their minds."

Trina was aware he was thinking of his mother and she said lightly:

"They should have had a Nanny like mine who always said: 'Beauty's only skin-deep and looks don't last, so make the best of them while you can!'"

The Marquis laughed.

"I am sure my Nanny said equally deflating things but with a masculine slant to them."

"Nannies are always practical and down-to-earth," Trina smiled, "and now I must be going. They will be wondering at the Château what has happened to me."

"Why are you alone?" the Marquis enquired. "Surely the *Comte* should be accompanying you, both last night and tonight."

"He is with his grandmother who is not well."

"Then his loss is my gain!" the Marquis observed. "I should have been very disappointed if I had not found you here, and very piqued, if that is the right word, if you had not been alone."

"Then perhaps I have been some compensation for the fact that you are not sitting at the green-baize tables, as I imagined you would be, with a lovely lady on either side, helping you challenge the Goddess of Fortune."

"Your imagination runs away with you, Lady Sherington," the Marquis said dryly. "I seldom gamble, and actually, although it may surprise you, I am going to Monte Carlo to visit a friend who is in ill-health, and who particularly desires my company."

"Then I hope she is also very pretty," Trina said before she could prevent herself.

Once again she was sparring with the Marquis as she had done the night before, and as she put it to herself, some devil within her wanted to provoke him.

She had risen as she spoke and the Marquis rose too.

"I see," he said in an amused voice, "that you are determined to turn me into a rake. Very well, Lady Sherington, I am only too prepared to play the part you have assigned to me."

Trina looked up at him, wondering how she could reply to this assertion and wanting to say something witty.

Then to her astonishment before she could speak, the Marquis's arms went round her and he pulled her against him.

Before she could realise what was happening, before she had time even to raise her hands to ward him off, his lips came down on hers and held her captive.

She was so astounded that for a moment she did not even struggle against him.

She was still because through sheer surprise her mind no longer seemed to function.

Then as she thought his lips were hard and being kissed was not what she had expected it to be, his arms tightened and it was impossible to fight herself free.

Suddenly she found herself surrendering to his mastery in a manner she could not explain.

Something strange and very wonderful seemed to move up through her breasts, into her throat, and to vibrate from her lips against his.

It gave her sensations she had never known she was capable of feeling.

It was also so wonderful, so perfect that she knew it was what she had heard in the song of the nightingales.

She felt as if the Marquis carried her up into the sky towards the stars, and they were one with the moonlight rippling on the river, the trees, the flowers and the view that stretched in the darkness away into the horizon.

She vibrated to a rapture for which he had said there were no words. It was a wonder and a glory which moved from the sky onto his lips and made her a part of him.

Only when it seemed that time had ceased to exist and a few minutes or several centuries had passed the Marquis raised his head.

With a little cry that was hardly audible, and yet came from the very depths of her being, Trina fought herself free of his arms.

Then she was running from him, speeding across the lawn with a swiftness that would have been impossible in anyone who was not very young.

She reached the Château.

Without thinking she ran to the open window by which she had left the Salon and only then was she conscious that her heart was thumping so violently in her breast that she could not breathe.

To her relief the lights were still glowing, but the room was empty. Susi must have gone to bed.

Because she was exhausted by her headlong flight, Trina sank down into a chair. Her breath was coming in uneven gasps from between her lips and she tried to control it.

Yet she knew what she had felt when the Marquis kissed her was something from which she could never escape, even if she never saw him again.

He had captured a part of her which she could never regain.

Chapter Five

TRINA AWOKE in the morning to think: 'How dare he kiss me!' Then because she could not help it, she whispered: "It was wonderful!"

Although quite a number of young men had tried to kiss her in Rome, she had kept them at arms' length and decided firmly in her own mind that she would never be kissed on the lips until she was in love.

The Marquis had taken her by surprise and she thought that ordinarily she would have not only struggled against him, but been extremely angry at his impertinence.

But she could not forget the wonder he had evoked in her and the way he made her feel as if he carried her towards the stars and that with his lips he drew her heart from her body and she became a part of him.

"I shall never see him again," she told herself.

She felt it was true that she had lost a rapture and enchantment that was his and his alone.

Because she was afraid of her own thoughts, she dressed quickly and ran downstairs to find her mother and the *Comte* were already having breakfast.

"You did not come to say goodnight to me," Susi said reproachfully.

"I thought you might be asleep," Trina replied.

She knew the truth was that after what she had felt with the Marquis, it would have been impossible to talk to anybody or to discuss any subject except him.

"Today, after we have been riding," the *Comte* said, "I am going to tell the Marchioness that the Elixir is arriving tonight and we can demonstrate its powers tomorrow."

Susi looked at him as if she was surprised at the urgency in his voice.

"If you want the truth," he said, "I wish we had not embarked on this particular adventure."

"I feel that too," Susi said. "At the same time, I know how much it means to you."

"I suppose it is necessary," the *Comte* said, "but even the Castle seems to have shrunk in importance."

Trina was well aware what he was trying to say: that the only thing which mattered was his love for Susi, and that he wanted her for his wife.

At the same time she could understand her mother's reluctance to allow him to sacrifice so much.

Trina was sure she was right in thinking that the *Comte* had never in his whole life been in love as he was now, and she knew that happiness would be a compensation for almost everything else.

Yet she understood too how much the history of their forebears meant to the noblemen both of France and Italy. It was part of their blood, and part too of the very air they breathed.

The *Comte* had been brought up to believe that his background was interwoven with his character and his personality, and it would be as difficult to divorce him from the Castle as it would be from a wife.

'If only I could find a solution,' Trina thought, 'then everything would be perfect.'

Perfection was however, something few people found in this world, and she told herself she had no magic wand to make her mother and the *Comte* live happily ever after.

At the same time, the sun was shining and they were both very much in love.

Trina watched them ride away on two of the *Comte*'s superb horses and felt as she was left behind, rather like Cinderella.

But there was still a great deal for her to do, if the Elixir was to be ready by tomorrow and she ran up the steps and into the Still-room to find that the *Comte* had left the apothecary's bottle which she had asked him for.

In fact, there were two of them, both very old, one of a deep amber glass which seemed to hold a faint touch of the sun in it, and the other made of the black crystal that she knew was used for the special products produced in Grasse.

She had found in the *Comte*'s Library, a *Catalogue de Parfumerie de la Fabrique*, 'furnished to the principal foreign Courts.'

In it were listed pots made of faience, pipeclay, porcelain, glass and crystal which contained pommades extracted from flowers, creams for the complexion made from snails, cucumber and alabaster, and wax for the moustache.

There were also flasks made of crystal or black glass which contained hazelnuts, Macasser water, Russian leather water and of course, lavender water.

Trina had thought that perhaps they should procure some of these age-old recipes for beauty to please the Marchioness.

There had, however, been no time to concentrate on anything except the Elixir and she decided the amber bottle would be most suitable, especially as it had an amusing little silver top which depicted a fawn dancing.

There were just one or two more ingredients that Trina wanted to introduce into what she had already distilled.

Two of them were very ancient herbs which the *Comte* had told her had been planted in the garden of the Castle at the time of Catherine di Medici.

There had been then a great interest in beauty products because Queen Catherine was so desperately jealous of the King's mistress, Diane de Poitiers.

Her beauty and the fact that she never appeared to grow older were attributed to witchcraft, but the real reason was that she bathed in cold water and preferred plain food and fresh vegetables to the heavy, over-rich meals that were fashionable at the Court.

'I wonder what the Marchioness eats?' Trina thought, and suspected as Susi had said she was slimming, that it was not the right things.

"Perhaps we could include suggestions for a health-giving and beautifying diet with the Elixir," she ruminated as she chopped up the herbs.

Then she smiled because she was concentrating on the Marchioness's beauty as if she had a personal interest in effecting for her what she craved.

"If we make her feel better, that automatically will improve her appearance, and we will not feel so guilty about the money," Trina told herself.

She knew, although Susi had not said so, that it went against her intrinsic honesty and frankness to deceive anyone, even a woman as stupid as the Marchioness.

"We are saving her from worse things," Trina said firmly, "and that is a good deed, whatever anyone might think."

The herbs were prepared and ready to be added to the rest of the Elixir by the time Susi and the *Comte* returned, and Trina tidied herself and went to the Salon to join them.

She began to open the door and as she did so, she heard her own name and instinctively stood still.

"I have not mentioned it before," she heard her mother say in a low voice, "because I thought when you—saw Trina as she looked so like—me that you would fall in love—with her."

"Do you really believe that I love you only because of your looks—breathtaking though they are?" the *Comte* asked.

"I thought," Susi said as if he had not spoken, "that you would—realise that Trina can—give you—everything that I am unable to do."

"By that you mean money."

"Yes. Trina will be rich—very rich, and there would be no—difficulty about—keeping up the Castle, the grounds and all the other properties you—own."

There was silence for a moment. Then the *Comte* said:

"Look at me, Susi!"

"You are not attending to what I am saying to you," Susi cried.

"You have not said anything that you have not hinted at a dozen times, my darling. But as I know everything you think, everything you feel, I have known this was in your mind ever since Trina arrived in Paris."

"Then if you knew what I was—thinking, why can you not—understand that is what would be— best for you? That is what will—ultimately make you—happy."

The *Comte* laughed.

"I adore you!" he said. "In many ways you are incredibly foolish, and I think actually that is another reason why I love you so much. Do you really believe, my precious, that a man of my age does not know his mind or can transfer his heart from one woman to another because it is more expedient for him to do so?"

"There have been—many women—in your—life," Susi faltered.

"Many!" the *Comte* agreed, "but they have always disappointed me. I imagined it was because I expected too much; demanded that they should match the ideal which lies in a special shrine in my heart."

He paused for a moment before he added very softly:

"That was until I met you."

"Oh, Jean, why do you say such—perfect things to me?" Susi cried.

"Because I love you," he replied, "and because you love me. Because also, my adorable little goose, your daughter to me is only a pale reflection of you, and I am not prepared to accept second best!"

"I am—trying to—help you."

"I know, my sweetest, but it is a very amateur effort and from my point of view very ineffective."

"You are laughing at me!" Susi protested.

"Only because I love you so much for thinking of me rather than yourself. Can you imagine what it would be like if I did what you wanted, and you had to watch me loving Trina and doing all

125

the things with her I have planned that you and I would do together?"

"I should—try to be—glad for—your sake."

"You know that would be impossible, and when you were alone at night, you would want me as I want you. Oh, my lovely one, I adore you for thinking of me, but I am selfish enough to want to think of myself, and I know you are the only woman in the world who could possibly make me happy."

"Is that true? Really—true?"

"Of course it is true!"

"Oh, darling—I love—you so—much!"

There was silence and Trina knew that the *Comte* was kissing her mother.

She shut the door quietly and moved away with a smile on her face.

She too had been aware that Susi had planned that she and the *Comte* should be married so that he could share her fortune.

"Dearest Mama is so unworldly," Trina told herself, "and of course, she has never been in love before now, so she knows so little about it, and less about men."

She thought perhaps that was Susi's attraction for the *Comte*.

He would have been bored with a very young girl, but Susi intrigued him as a woman, and at the same time, her unsophistication and her purity was something he had never found previously in the life of gaiety and amusement he had led in Paris.

"They are perfectly suited!" Trina said to herself. "But Mama will never understand that much as I like him, I am not the least in love with Jean de Girone."

A little voice inside her asked her if there was not someone else she loved—a very different type of man—but she had no answer and was only sure that when they reached Paris there would be plenty of men provided by the *Duchesse* who would both amuse and interest her.

After dinner that evening she found herself wondering if she should go to the place where she had heard the nightingales. Then she thought it would be an anti-climax to be alone there after the two nights when she had talked with the Marquis.

She drew in her breath as she remembered how last night he had kissed her and it was agonising to think that perhaps tonight he was kissing someone else on the Riviera.

She told herself severely that she would be very foolish if she attached too much importance to his kiss.

She had teased and provoked him and he had retaliated in a manner she had not expected, merely because she was not as experienced in the art of flirtation as he thought her to be.

She was quite certain that the sophisticated women with whom he usually associated would have expected to be kissed if they were alone with such an attractive man, and would have thought it was merely a compliment to their beauty and their attractions.

How could the Marquis guess it was the first time she had ever been kissed or that it had made her feel a thousand wonderful emotions she had never even imagined?

She imagined that as he journeyed towards Monte Carlo early today he perhaps had thought with a cynical smile on his lips that he had scored off the *Comte* by kissing the woman of whom, at the moment, he was obviously enamoured.

The particular social set in London to which the Marquis belonged doubtless spent their time in this way when they were not watching their horses race each other's, or attempting to kill more pheasants than their friends.

'I mean nothing to him,' Trina thought, 'and by now he will already have forgotten me.'

She left the Salon but she did not go out into the garden.

Instead she went up to bed and quite unaccountably, after Susi had come to say goodnight to her, looking so radiantly happy that her eyes seemed to light the room, Trina cried herself to sleep.

———————————————————

The following morning the *Comte* was very business-like in his plans for the day.

"I have arranged with the Marchioness," he said, "that she will meet us in the Music Room at three o'clock. Until then there is a lot to do."

He saw that both Susi and Trina were listening to him and he went on:

"I have found several heavy and very beautiful tapestry screens with which I intend to encircle the chair in which Susi and you will sit."

"If they are heavy, that should prevent them from falling over by mistake, which would be disastrous!" Trina said.

"Exactly!" the *Comte* agreed. "Over the top to make a kind of box in which you will be enclosed there will be a Chinese shawl."

"I am—feeling rather frightened," Susi said. "You must tell me exactly what I have to do."

"I will seat you in the chair," the *Comte* said, "which, although it will not be obvious to anyone else, will be fastened to the floor so that you will not be frightened when it moves."

He smiled at her and went on:

"*Comte* Bernhard had a special spring by which he made the chair descend, but it will be quite easy for Trina waiting below to wind you down without your doing anything. Then when she seats herself in your place, you turn the handle which lifts the chair back into place."

"Supposing—it sticks—and I am not—strong enough?" Susi asked.

"I promise you it is very easy," the *Comte* replied, "and so that you will not be worried, I am going to take you there this morning and show you exactly what to do."

"I have been wondering about one thing," Trina said, "when we have finished you and I will be in the Music Room but Mama will be down below. How will you get both of us away from the Castle and back here?"

"I have thought of that," the *Comte* said. "You will stay with the Marchioness, telling her what effect the Elixir has had on you and how young you feel."

"I am sure I can be very eloquent on the subject," Trina said dryly.

"While you are doing that," the *Comte* said, "I will slip away and go to the room below. Susi and I will leave the Castle by the same way that you will enter it."

"How is that?" Trina asked.

"My magical ancestor thought of everything," the *Comte* replied. "When he disappeared from the Music Room through the floor, he wound the chair back into place, then left the Castle by an underground passage which comes out near the stables."

Trina's eyes sparkled.

"I want to see it."

"It is a very ingenious route of escape," the *Comte* said, "because even in those days, as now, the exit was concealed by shrubs. We can walk back to the Château through shrubberies where it will be impossible for anyone to see us from the Castle."

"It grows more and more exciting!" Trina exclaimed.

Only Susi made no effort to enthuse about the plans.

The *Comte* then took Susi off to show her the

way into the Castle and how to work the moving chair.

"I shall have time to show you, Trina," he said before he left, "when I put you in the room immediately after luncheon. Susi and I will arrive at the front door at about a quarter to three."

Trina understood that he was enjoying the plot, treating it as she had done at the beginning as a theatrical performance where everything must be on time and everybody have their right cue.

"What music are you going to play?" she enquired.

"Something loud to begin with," the *Comte* answered, "because as you anticipated the machinery might squeak a little. Then something soft and soothing while presumably the Elixir works and Susi is transformed into a young and beautiful maiden!"

Trina had found among her gowns two that were identical.

"I cannot imagine now why I ordered two exactly the same," she said. "But it was such a pretty model for the summer, that I suppose I got carried away, or else I thought it would save me the trouble of choosing something else."

"It is certainly exactly what we need," Susi said, "and they will require little alteration."

Actually Susi's lady's-maid had to let out for her the waist of Trina's gown by nearly two inches, but as there was a sash it did not show and if it was a little tight in the bodice she did not complain.

Trina made sure before luncheon that their hair was arranged in exactly the same way, and even the *Comte*, regarding them with a critical eye, could not find fault.

"Do you really—believe that no-one could—tell us apart?" Susi asked him.

"I should always know you," he answered, "but then, as you know, I am *fada* where you are concerned."

"Let us hope the Marchioness will not have the same powers," Susi said.

"How could she have?" the *Comte* answered. "They are exclusive to a Provençal and we are very zealous to make sure that outsiders do not encroach on our special magic."

They laughed, but Trina was sure it was very unlikely that anyone, especially a woman as stupid as the Marchioness, would notice any difference between her and Susi.

'The Marquis might be different,' she thought.

Then she told herself that he had believed her to be a married woman eighteen years older than she actually was!

'He is certainly not *fada*!' she thought scornfully.

At the same time, she was glad he was not to be present at the afternoon's performance.

* * *

Although Trina had told herself she did not suffer from nerves, she found her heart beating a little faster when after she and the *Comte* had reached the place beneath the Music Room, he left her there alone.

It had been an excitement walking through the shrubs, finding the entrance to the underground passage and creeping along it in a crouching position.

They entered the room through a secret place in the panelling. This too was very low as it was really only a space between two floors and not intended to be occupied.

In the centre of it was a strange contraption consisting of a wheel with iron struts stretching to the ceiling.

"It is quite easy to turn," the *Comte* said.

To demonstrate he rolled the wheel with his hands and the chair came down from above firmly fixed to a piece of the parquet flooring.

Trina watched fascinated, then said:

"You are quite sure there is nobody in the room above?"

"I locked the door after I had arranged the screens and the Chinese shawl over them."

"You think of everything!"

She peeped upwards but all she could see was darkness.

The *Comte* then made her sit in the chair while he turned the wheel that would lift her to the Music Room.

It was so well contrived that even after so many years, now that it had been oiled, it moved with very little effort.

133

There was just a slight click as the floor fitted into place, then the *Comte* wound her down again and Trina cried:

"How could *Comte* Bernhard have thought of anything so clever?"

"He was well in advance of his time and had a very inventive mind," the *Comte* answered, "and remember he was always propelled by an ardent desire to survive."

"There were so many enemies to be afraid of in those days!"

"Now we have only one," the *Comte* remarked wryly, "poverty!"

Trina thought for a moment. Then she said:

"I heard what Mama said to you last night. I knew it was in her mind, but she did not say anything to me."

"I have never known a woman as unselfish and with such a sweet character as your mother," the *Comte* said. "Are you surprised that having found her, I intend never to let her go?"

"I should be very angry if you did," Trina remarked. "And now that we can talk openly, I want to tell you that you are exactly the person she should marry."

"I am glad you approve of your future Stepfather!" the *Comte* smiled.

Trina laughed.

"You do not really seem old enough, but I accept you in that position with the greatest of pleasure!"

They both laughed without bothering to say

in words that neither of them had any desire for any other kind of relationship.

Then they hurried back to Susi.

Waiting for the music above to tell her that she must wind down the chair, Trina found herself offering up a little prayer that everything would be successful.

The *Comte* was so charming, she thought. He deserved happiness just as her mother did.

"I will help him, I will help him in every way I can," she vowed.

The *Comte* was aware as they drove over the drawbridge which would lead them to the centre of the Castle, that Susi was trembling.

"Please do not be frightened, my darling," he said. "If you are, I shall call the whole thing off. I cannot bear you to be upset or worried."

He could not have said anything which would have made Susi more resolute in her desire to help him.

"I am only—afraid that I may—fail you," she answered, "but I—want to help you—I want to do everything you ask of me."

"That is easy," the *Comte* replied. "I want you to love me!"

He saw the light come into her eyes and knew as she stepped out of the carriage, that she had a new confidence in herself.

The Marchioness was waiting for them in the

Hall and was looking excited except that her face was so plastered with cosmetics that it was almost impossible to see what she really did look like.

Her hair was a glaring, rather hard gold that in contrast made Susi's look like the sunshine in the spring, and her eye-lashes were heavily mascaraed.

"You have brought the Elixir?" she asked, although she was well aware of what the *Comte* carried in his hand, carefully wrapped in paper.

"I have it here," he replied.

They walked towards the Music Room and Susi saw that the *Comte* had drawn the curtains slightly so as not to admit too much sunlight.

The room was also decorated with great vases of flowers which scented the air.

"How pretty this room is!" the Marchioness exclaimed. "I do not think I have been in it before."

"Today it is the right atmosphere for the experiment we are about to make," the *Comte* said. "As I have already told you, Lady Sherington will sit in the chair surrounded by screens. She will drink the Elixir and we must have perfect quiet and peace for it to work. The only sound will be the music I shall play."

"You think that is important?" the Marchioness asked.

"Very!" the *Comte* replied seriously. "Any shock or disturbance might have the opposite effect to what we intend."

"I understand!" the Marchioness said.

Susi looked at her and thought that in her eagerness she was even more pathetic than she had been when they had first met.

There was still a great deal of beauty in her face, but there was no character and very little personality behind it.

'It must be terrible,' Susi thought, 'to spend the last years of one's life only looking back at one's youth. There must be things to do which will help other people and even things to learn however old we become. How can she be so foolish as to waste her life on a wild goose-chase?'

But she knew that was something she could not say.

Then as the *Comte* unwrapped the amber-coloured glass flask, the Marchioness gave a shrill cry of delight and excitement.

"So that is the Elixir of Youth! The Elixir I have been seeking for so long! Why do we waste time? Let me drink it now!"

"No," the *Comte* said firmly. "That would be a mistake. I want to prove to you what it should do, although of course, I must tell you that as you are older than Lady Sherington you cannot expect one glass to work as quickly where you are concerned."

"Of course, I understand that," the Marchioness said.

"Come and sit here," the *Comte* suggested indicating the chair he had chosen where the Marchioness was facing the light while Susi, when she was not sitting in the chair, had her back to it.

"Yes, of course, I will do exactly what you tell me," the Marchioness agreed. "And as you have the Elixir for me, *Comte*, I have something for you."

As she spoke she drew from her bag a cheque made out for £10,000 and held it out towards him.

For a moment the *Comte* hesitated, and Susi knew that his instinct was to refuse it, to be honest and say that after all what they offered her would not work as the Marchioness wished it to do, and tell her to keep her money.

But even as she held her breath she knew the *Comte* had remembered Antonio di Casapellio waiting in Italy to hypnotise and rob the poor, foolish woman.

"Thank you," he said.

The abrupt way he spoke told Susi just how much he disliked now, at the very last moment, what he was doing.

He put the flask down on a table where there was already a crystal wine glass on a silver tray. Then he took the cheque and thrust it into his pocket.

"You are ready to drink the Elixir, Lady Sherington?" he asked Susi.

"I am—longing to do so," Susi replied. "I am thirty-six and afraid that old age is already beginning to creep towards me. It will be wonderful to be really—young again."

The Marchioness gave a deep sigh.

"That is what I am longing for; to know one can look in a mirror without shuddering, to see a man's eyes light up when I appear, and know that every woman who looks at me is envious."

Her voice throbbed with emotion as she went on:

"I can still hear the cheers of the crowd whenever I appeared in London. There was always a hundred people or more waiting outside Clevedon House when I left in the morning, and riding down Rotten Row was like a Royal procession."

Susi had heard her say this before, but she listened wondering if the Marchioness ever thought of anything else but her triumphs of many years ago.

"Do you know what the Emperor of France, Louis Napoleon, said to me the first time I went to Paris . . . ?" the Marchioness began, then she stopped. "I can tell you all this later. Please, *Comte*, do not let us waste any more time. Give Lady Sherington the Elixir."

The *Comte* poured from the amber flask, then with the glass in his hands he said to Susi:

"You must sit in the chair and compose yourself. Keep your eyes closed."

Susi walked to the chair set between the screens and when she was seated she took the glass from the *Comte's* hands and drank it. He immediately closed the screen around her and pulled the embroidered shawl into place.

Then without speaking he walked very quietly across the room and sat down at the piano.

As he struck the first chords he knew that Trina would know what she had to do.

She had, in fact, put her hands some minutes earlier on the wheel.

Although they were very faint, she could hear the sound of voices above and the slight scrape which she knew meant that the *Comte* had put the screen in place.

Now slowly, without hurry, as he had instructed her, she turned the wheel and immediately the chair came down from above with Susi sitting in it.

They smiled at each other, but the *Comte* had told them very firmly that they must not speak.

Trina took Susi's place and immediately the chair began to rise.

She held her breath in case something should go wrong until it fitted, as *Comte* Bernhard, those centuries ago, had intended, precisely and accurately into its place in the floor above.

She felt the agitation which had made her hold her breath subside as she listened to the music the *Comte* was playing on the piano.

It made her think of the nightingales and the song of love they had sung to her that first night when to her astonishment she had found the Marquis standing behind her.

She was thinking of how handsome he was,

how broad-shouldered and in a way, overpowering, when the music stopped and she heard the *Comte*'s footsteps coming towards her across the room.

She kept her eyes shut and now he was moving away the screens and she knew that he was standing in front of her.

"Wake up, Lady Sherington!" he said quietly.

Trina blinked her eyes as if she had actually been sleeping, and the *Comte* put out his hand and drew her from the chair.

"Let us look at you," he said, "and you must also tell us what you are feeling."

He drew her from between the screens and Trina saw the Marchioness staring at her with a rapt expression on her face.

Then she felt as if her heart stopped beating, for standing a little distance behind the Marchioness in the entrance to the room where the *Comte* had been unable to see him from the piano, was the Marquis!

It seemed to Trina as if everything turned a somersault including her heart and she had no idea what she should do about it.

Quite unaware that the Marquis was there, the *Comte* was leading her towards his mother.

"Now we shall know, Your Ladyship," he said, "how successful the Elixir has been."

He thought as he spoke that even anyone as stupid as the Marchioness could not fail to see the difference between Susi's and Trina's ages.

The purple shadows and the little wrinkles at the corners of her eyes which Trina had put in so painstakingly were, of course, missing.

But it was obvious to him that there was something very young and spring-like about Trina that made her seem, for the moment, as if she was Persephone come back from the darkness of Hades.

"There *is* a difference," the Marchioness said, in an ecstatic voice. "I can see it! The lines have gone from her face. They have really disappeared!"

"How do you feel?" the *Comte* enquired of Trina.

She had while she had been waiting below, rehearsed what she was to say, but now because the Marquis was listening, she found it difficult to speak.

"At first I . . . felt strange . . . a little dizzy," she said after a moment's hesitation. "but then . . . it was as if . . . something alive was moving within me . . . it was . . . strange . . . and yet exciting . . . and now I feel as if . . . I . . . could dance and sing . . . because I am . . . happy."

"That is exactly what I was told you would feel," the *Comte* said.

"It works! It really works!" the Marchioness cried. "Shall I take it now or wait?"

"I think it would be wise in your case, to wait," the *Comte* replied, "at least until tonight. It would perhaps work better if you slept longer, to give the Elixir a chance to work."

"I will take it tonight," the Marchioness agreed.

"But only one wine-glassful each day," the *Comte* said. "What is in the flask should last for a week or longer."

"Yes, yes," the Marchioness cried. "One glass— but I shall be impatient if it does not work at once."

"Too much might do more harm than good."

"Then it shall be just one glass," the Marchioness said meekly.

"I am sure you would like Lady Sherington to sit down and talk to you for a little while," the *Comte* said. "There must be many questions you will want to ask her, and so I shall leave you."

He kissed the Marchioness's hand, then as he walked toward the door, Trina stole a glance in the same direction.

To her inexpressible relief the Marquis was no longer there.

'Perhaps I dreamed it,' she thought, 'but he seemed real, so very real.'

Nevertheless she was afraid.

The Marchioness, however, was ready to begin her questions.

"Tell me what you feel," she begged. "I am so intrigued to learn how it works."

Trina explained, and the Marchioness asked:

"Did you have a creeping feeling under your skin, as if it were more active than it had been before?"

"It is very difficult to put into words," Trina replied.

She knew as she spoke that the real difficulty

was that the Marquis had upset her by his sudden appearance.

Why had he come back?

Surely there cannot have been another fall of stones on the railway line? It could not be to see her—she was certain of that. Then, why? Why?

All the time the Marchioness was talking, going over and over the same ground, but she found it impossible to concentrate on anything.

It gave her a feeling of unutterable relief when about ten minutes later the Marchioness, as if she was aware there was nothing more to discuss, rose to her feet.

"I am going to take the Elixir of Youth very carefully to my bedroom," she said. "It would be disastrous if the servants knocked it over by mistake. Thank you, Lady Sherington. Will you come and see me tomorrow? Then we can compare notes, and you will be able to see what this wonderful potion has done for me!"

"Yes, of course," Trina agreed.

"Thank you again, from the bottom of my heart," the Marchioness said, "and tomorrow morning, if I look like you, I shall be the happiest woman in the world."

Clutching the amber bottle closely against her breast, she went from the room without waiting for her.

Trina was aware that although the *Comte* had said he would return for her, it would be impossible for him to do so quickly.

It would take him nearly a quarter-of-an-hour

to drive away so that the servants would see him go and then another fifteen minutes at least, to walk back through the shrubs to the hidden passage and take Susi back to the Château.

"I will walk," Trina told herself. "After all, if I go through the gardens no-one will be surprised."

She had almost reached the door of the Music-Room when she remembered that Susi would have left her gloves and her hand-bag on a chair before she had been enclosed by the screen.

Trina retrieved them and, holding them in her hand, walked from the Music-Room. Only as she reached the passage outside did she start and draw in her breath.

Waiting for her, looking very large and over-powering, was the Marquis!

Chapter Six

FOR A moment Trina could only stand looking at the Marquis, and she knew that he was angry.

"I want to speak to you, Lady Sherington."

"I was just . . . going home."

He did not answer but they walked away down the passage and he opened the door into the Library.

Because there was nothing else she could do, she walked in ahead of him and moved towards the fireplace.

She thought as she did so, how many hours she and her mother had spent poring over the books on herbs in their efforts to make the Elixir of Youth for the Marchioness.

Then she could think of nothing but that the

Marquis seemed very large and overpowering as he walked slowly to join her on the hearth-rug.

"I want an explanation," he said, "and it had better be a good one!"

"I do not know what you mean," Trina replied. "I thought you had gone away."

"I had," he answered, "but when I arrived in Nice yesterday it was to learn from the newspapers that the friend I was to see in Monte Carlo had died, so I returned—obviously at an inopportune moment."

The way he spoke made Trina aware that he was not only suspicious of what had been happening while he was away, but also extremely annoyed.

Because she was nervous, she said quickly:

"I want to . . . return to the Château and I am sure the *Comte* will answer all your . . . questions if you wish to . . . put them to him."

"I prefer to put them to you."

"I have nothing to tell you."

"That is not true, and you know it!"

Trina did not answer and after a moment he said:

"I was aware that my mother came to Provence to find herbs which she thought would make her young again, and I imagine that is what she was carrying when I saw her leaving the Music Room."

He paused then continued:

"But I should be interested to know, Lady Sherington, what she paid for the flask she carried in her hand and how you were deceiving her in coming out of that contraption which was obviously a part of some conjurer's magic trick."

Trina thought he had come uncomfortably near the truth and lifting her chin a little, she replied:

"I think your mother can give you a very adequate explanation."

"First, the *Comte*, then my mother," the Marquis said. "I am asking you, Lady Sherington."

"I have nothing to tell you."

"Why? Are you ashamed of what you have done?"

"Not in the slightest, and I only took part in the experiment . . ."

"An experiment?" the Marquis interrupted. "Now we are getting somewhere! What sort of experiment? And why were you hidden behind those screens?"

He had raised his voice to speak in an unmistakably aggressive tone.

"I think, My Lord," Trina said quietly, "I have every right to refuse to be cross-examined by you, and I therefore repeat that I am going back to the Château. If you wish to come with me, you are of course, at liberty to do so."

As she spoke she glanced at the Marquis and saw his eyes narrow. Then she looked away again, conscious that her heart was beating uncomfortably in her breast.

"My mother had been duped by one charlatan after another," the Marquis said, "but I was not expecting the *Comte* de Girone, and least of all you, to be added to the list of those who have extracted money from her, under false pretences."

Trina longed to reply that neither she nor the *Comte* had done anything of the sort, but she was uncomfortably aware there was a cheque for £10,000 in his pocket.

"Who are you?" the Marquis demanded unexpectedly, "and what are you getting out of this?"

Trina looked at him in surprise and he went on:

"I do not believe you are Lady Sherington. My mother told me she was thirty-six and a widow. It is completely impossible for you to be that age."

"What makes you so . . . sure of that?"

"Now that I see you in the daylight," the Marquis replied, "I would be prepared to wager a very large sum that you are half the age you pretend to be."

It flashed through Trina's mind that when she had thought he was perceptive, she had been right.

Because she knew she had annoyed him, she said with what she hoped was almost a simper:

"Your Lordship is very . . . complimentary."

"And I would also be prepared," the Marquis said slowly, "to swear that when I kissed you, it was for the first time."

Now the colour flooded over Trina's face and because she wanted only to escape from the penetrating expression in his eyes, she turned towards the door.

"I refuse to go on with this . . . conversation."

She meant to sound proud and dignified, but instead her words came out in a soft, shy little voice.

She was already moving when the Marquis seized hold of her wrist and brought her to an abrupt stop.

"Answer me!" he commanded. "Who are you? Are you some actress the *Comte* has engaged to play a part in defrauding my mother?"

"Let me go!"

The Marquis's fingers only tightened.

"You will go when you have answered me, and not before!"

"Then you may have to wait here all night," Trina retorted.

"Doubtless like when you were waiting for the nightingales, you will prove yourself a very skilled performer."

His voice was so cynical and bitter that Trina longed to reply that she had not been acting then.

The wonder of his kiss, the strange sensations he had evoked in her, swept over her to make her feel that she could not go on prevaricating. She must tell him the truth and ask him to forgive her.

Then she knew she could not be so disloyal to the *Comte*. She knew also that once the Marquis knew she had in fact, been deceiving his mother, he would never speak to her again.

151

Because she was upset, she tried once again to free herself, saying:

"Let me go! You have no right to keep me here."

"I think I have every right," the Marquis contradicted. "You have conspired to make a fool of my mother and therefore you will either tell me the truth now or I shall keep you here until you do!"

"Do not be so ridiculous!" Trina exclaimed. "Those sort of threats are only empty words!"

"I will prove that they are meaningful, unless you tell me what I want to hear."

"Which I have no intention of doing," Trina replied. "When the *Comte* returns for me, which he will do in a very short time, you can hardly tell him that you are keeping me as a hostage."

"You sound as if you are certain he will not wish to lose you. Is he your lover?"

Trina did not stop to think before she flared furiously:

"No, of course not! How can you . . . suggest such a thing?"

"From the way he spoke about you to my mother, there was no doubt he was enamoured of you. I therefore presumed that he has had to let his Castle since he needs the money, and you are assisting him to get it."

"You have a very active imagination, My Lord," Trina said in a voice which she hoped was as sarcastic as his.

"You certainly stimulate it," he replied. "It is

not hard to see the way you have been plotting."

He paused and Trina was wondering how she could get away from him.

He still held her wrist in what was almost a vise-like grip, and she knew that, even if she was free, long before she could reach the door and open it, he would be able to stop her.

"I think really all I need to know," the Marquis went on, "is how much my mother paid you to produce that herbal rubbish and to deceive her by some mumbo-jumbo which took place in a make-shift magician's cabinet."

He was getting nearer and nearer to the truth, Trina thought.

But for the *Comte*'s sake she must not let him know the existence of Susi or indeed the enormous sum of money his mother had paid for what she believed to be an Elixir of Youth.

"If you are determined not to let me go," she said coldly, "we . . . might sit down. I am finding it extremely tiring standing here arguing for no reason."

"There is plenty of reason," the Marquis answered, "but I have a better idea."

Pulling her by the wrist he walked towards the door, opened it and drawing her with him, started to walk down the passage.

Trina hoped he was taking her to the front door, perhaps to throw her out.

But she could feel the waves of anger emanating from him which did not give her any real hope of escape.

They walked some way along the passage which she knew led to the back of the Castle, and while she was puzzling as to where they were heading the Marquis seemed sure of himself.

She thought if they met any of the servants they would think it strange that the Marquis should be dragging her by the wrist, but they met no-one.

Trina had the idea, although she was not sure, that they were in a part of the Castle that was not often in use.

Soon they came to a stairway leading downwards, which was wide enough for two people to walk side by side and the Marquis started down it.

Only as they descended lower and still lower, did Trina ask:

"Where are you taking me? This is ridiculous! The *Comte* will be expecting me at the Château."

"Then he will be disappointed," the Marquis snapped.

It struck Trina that the air was cooler, in fact almost cold, after the heat of the rooms they had just left.

There were still a few steps ahead, when she stopped dead.

"I am going no further!" she said. "Let me go back, or I will scream for help!"

The Marquis looked around as if he would draw her attention to the ancient stone walls which Trina suddenly realised were bare and not decorated with tapestries or pictures, as in other parts of the Castle.

Quite suddenly she remembered that she had seen this particular staircase before, when the *Comte* had been showing Susi and her around the Castle the first afternoon they had arrived.

"That is the way to the dungeons," he had said. "I will show them to you sometime, but not now. There are so many other things to see."

Now she was afraid.

"Why are you . . . bringing me . . . here?" she asked and her voice trembled.

"You will see," the Marquis said ominously.

Although she tried to resist him, he pulled her down the last few steps.

Now as they moved forward with the light coming only through arrow-slits in the walls, she saw ahead, as she had half-expected, a huge oak door with iron hinges and an enormous square lock.

"This is the . . . way to the . . . dungeons," she said.

"I am aware of that," the Marquis retorted, "and I think you will find it a salutary experience to be incarcerated in one until you are prepared to tell me what I intend to hear."

"You are mad!" Trina exclaimed. "You cannot really be behaving in such a crazy manner!"

"It may seem crazy to you," the Marquis replied, "but if you use mediaeval methods yourself, then you must expect mediaeval punishments!"

He stopped, still holding her by the wrist, turned the key in the lock, and she saw ahead of her more steps going down to a lower floor.

The dim light coming through the arrow-slits revealed chains fastened at intervals along the walls which must once have been used to tether prisoners.

She gave a little gasp, and the Marquis said:

"I am afraid you will not find it very comfortable, but when you are ready to tell me the truth you will see there is a bell attached to a rope on the right-hand side of the door. Ring it, and I will come and set you free."

Completely bemused by what he was saying, Trina looked towards the rope, and she was about to speak when the Marquis added:

"If you think to attract attention by ringing it or by shouting, let me inform you it is quite impossible for anyone who is not in this part of the Castle, to hear you. I hope you enjoy your solitude, Lady Sherington!"

He took a step backwards as he spoke, and almost before Trina could realise what was happening, he had moved back through the heavy oak door and shut it behind him.

She heard the key turn in the lock, then his footsteps crossing the stone floor and walking up the stairs.

She could hardly believe he had actually gone or had locked her in the dungeon. It must be some horrible dream from which she could not awaken.

Then there was a damp smell that was inescapable, and she felt cold on her face and hands.

The ceiling in the dungeon was quite high and

the arrow-slits were at the very top of the walls which she told herself must be just at ground level.

For a moment she contemplated beating on the door and screaming. Then she knew it would not only be undignified but useless.

From what she had seen of the Castle, she was sure that the part in which she was now imprisoned was at the back.

It was also beyond the stables where the *Comte* and Susi would have emerged from the hidden passage, to walk home through the shrubberies.

There would, therefore, be no-one to hear her, however loudly she screamed and, as the Marquis had said, no-one inside would suspect for one moment where she was.

"I will not give in to him!" Trina told herself defiantly.

She wanted to hate him for what he had done to her—yet at the same time, she could not help feeling a sneaking respect for the man who was so determined and so dominating.

In a way, although she hated to admit it, he was perfectly right. They were defrauding his mother, and he was protecting her as only a good son would do.

"I am making excuses for him," Trina murmured.

Even so, just as she had sparred provocatively with him ever since they had met, she wanted now to defy him and, if it was humanly possible, to beat him at his own game.

The question was how?

She was quite certain he was determined not to let her out until she told him the truth and it would be impossible to lie convincingly enough to deceive him.

And yet, Trina asked herself, how could she give in tamely? How could she ring the bell and say:

"I am sorry. I helped the *Comte* take £10,000 off your foolish mother, for some herbs we told her were the Elixir of Youth, and which she thinks have changed me from the appearance of a woman of thirty-six, to how I look now!"

"I will not do it! I will not!" Trina told herself defiantly. "If I do he will be more sure of himself than he is already, and even more overpowering."

Because she felt cold, she walked down the steps and crossed the stone floor.

She looked at the heavy, rusty chains and thought perhaps she was lucky he had not used them to fasten her to the wall.

She could not help thinking of the prisoners who had sat here year after year in abject despair, gradually losing their hope of being rescued.

Vaguely at the back of her mind she thought she had once heard that the only time they were allowed to ring the bell was when one of their number had died.

She shuddered at the thought of it.

Then she told herself the Marquis was only

frightening her because he was angry and because he was determined to get his own way.

'I shall not die,' she thought, 'but I shall catch a cold which will be extremely unbecoming.'

As she walked the whole length of the dungeon and back again she thought imaginatively that the prisoners who had once been incarcerated there were telling her that it was hopeless to try to fight against the inevitable.

She would have to do what the Marquis wanted even though doubtless he would gloat over her helplessness and his victory, in what had really been an unequal contest.

"How could we have anticipated for one moment," Trina asked, "that his friend would die, and he would come back when he was not wanted?"

At the same time, she could not help remembering that if he had not done so, she would never have seen him again.

She was sure that now the *Comte* had the £10,000 and was anxious that no-one should realise that she existed, he would arrange for her to leave for Paris immediately.

She wondered what he would think when he returned to the Castle to find she was not there.

She had a feeling that the Marquis would tell him that he had no idea where she had gone. It would be the obvious thing to say.

"Lady Sherington? Oh, I think she walked home some time ago. You will doubtless find her in the garden."

The *Comte* would believe him and it would certainly never enter his mind that she was locked in the dungeon of the Castle.

There was obviously no hope of being rescued that way.

"I shall have to give in," she sighed.

Then it suddenly struck her that *Comte* Bernhard might have imagined a day might come when he would be a prisoner in his own Castle.

In which case, surely, as he had escape routes everywhere else he would have put one here?

There was a light in Trina's eyes that had not been there before! When first she had moved slowly and rather hopelessly, she now walked quickly around the walls, noting every detail.

The arrow-slits were all on the West side, which meant that the East wall was doubtless an interior wall of the building, while the North wall which was opposite the door, was blank.

She stared at it wondering if there was any place where *Comte* Bernhard could have concealed a catch or lever such as she had seen in other parts of the Castle.

But there had always been ornamentation of some sort to hide his clever contraptions, a carving in a panel, a marble fireplace, or a place on the floor like they had just used in the Music Room.

Trina touched one or two of the bricks. They were cold and slightly damp and she thought that if there was a mechanism of any sort, it would have rusted hopelessly by now.

She however looked at everything, scrutinising every detail carefully and trying to think where a secret passage could be hidden.

She found herself almost praying that she would find an escape because it would discomfit the Marquis and he would be astonished when he came back, expecting her to be penitent and apologetic, to find the dungeon empty.

'Perhaps then he will believe not only in the Elixir, but that I am Lady Sherington, and that I am thirty-six years of age,' she thought with a smile.

She went on searching only to feel as helpless as the prisoners must have felt years ago. She tried the West wall, and that too was damp.

'I shall have to give in,' she thought despairingly.

But some obstinacy made her refuse to acknowledge defeat until she absolutely had to.

Defiantly she crossed the dungeon floor.

As she touched the East wall she found it was dry. That at least gave her the hope that if there was any mechanism there it might still be in working order.

There seemed to be no reason to think any of the bricks were different from any others, but she moved along the wall methodically, looking for a crack or anything that might suggest a hidden spring or lever.

She had almost reached the end and was back again at the North wall when her foot caught in one of the chains. She stumbled over it, only preventing herself with an effort, from falling to her knees.

'It is no use,' she thought, 'I am cold, and when it grows dark I shall be frightened if I am here alone.'

To save herself from falling she had caught at the chain where it was attached to the wall, and now she felt as if it gave a little.

An idea struck her. She pulled.

It seemed loose and because she was curious and it was a last forlorn hope, she pulled as hard as she could with both her hands.

Then she gave a little cry of excitement. The chain came towards her and with it part of the wall to which it was attached.

It moved slowly and then there was a space about three feet high and two feet wide.

"A secret passage!" Trina cried. "This is what I have been looking for, and now the Marquis will look foolish."

She sank down on her knees and stared inside.

She expected it to be dark, but strangely enough she saw a faint light in the distance.

She was well aware that any passage that had not been used for a long time might be dangerous not only because it might collapse on top of her, but also because the air could be poisonous.

However she told herself that she was prepared to risk almost anything rather than surrender to the Marquis as she had thought she would have to do.

She began to crawl through the opening, conscious that there was very little air, but telling herself if it was too foul she would go back.

The passage was wider than she had thought it would be. In fact, once she was inside there was plenty of room to move except that its height was no more than about three feet.

She crawled on, finding the earth on which she was moving was dry, and all the time there was a faint light ahead.

It was only a distance of perhaps twelve feet but it seemed a long way and she was in fact, rather frightened, although she would not admit it, of becoming unconscious due to the bad air.

Suddenly she found herself in a high circular cave, for it could be nothing else, and the light in it came from an arrow-slit high up near the roof.

Trina's first feeling was one of disappointment. This was not a passage leading her outside by which she could escape as she had hoped, but ending in another part of the Castle from which there seemed to be no exit.

It was, however, difficult to be certain because there had been a fall of stones in the centre of the cave, and if there was, in fact, an exit on the other side, she would have to crawl over or round the rubbish to reach it.

Then as she looked at what lay in her way she saw it was not a pile of stones as she had first thought, but some material which had over the ages crumbled to become nothing but dust.

She pushed it with her fingers and as she did

so, discovered there was something hard underneath.

Again she thought it must be stones or earth from the ceiling, until she saw something glitter.

She stared, moved a little more of the dust and saw that what she was looking at was a plate, round but dark, and yet there was no doubt that it was made of some substance which, old though it was, could still glitter in the light from the arrow-slit.

Then an idea struck her and the words she had read to her mother when she had not been listening, about *Comte* Bernhard, came back to her:

" . . . has contrived by powers beyond mortal men to hide his weapons, his treasures, and his women from the eyes of those who sought them!"

Trina gave a little cry, then she was urgently pushing away the dust of the pile in front of her with both her hands.

It took her a little time to realise the magnitude of what she had found, and by that time her hands were filthy, the front of her white gown was grey from the dust, and her cheeks were smudged.

But her eyes were shining like stars and with some difficulty she turned and crawled back the way she had come.

Only when she reached the dungeon did the

excitement of her discovery make her feel weak and she sat for a moment on the floor, propped against the secret opening, gasping for breath, at the same time, saying a prayer of thankfulness which seemed to come spontaneously to her lips.

"Thank You... God. Thank You... thank You! Now Mama can marry the *Comte* and there will be no more problems, no more worries."

She felt curiously near to tears from the very wonder of it.

Then she started to her feet and running down the dungeon she grasped the rope attached to the bell and pealed it again and again.

She was impatient, and when the Marquis did not appear immediately she thought perhaps he had changed his mind and was determined to leave her alone until she was as humble and compliant as he wanted her to be.

Then with a leap of her heart she heard his footsteps coming down the stairs, and a moment later the key was turning in the lock.

As he opened the door Trina pushed her way through the opening as if she could not wait.

"Take me back... take me back," she cried before he could speak, "and I will tell you everything... everything! But I must go to the Château... first."

Only as she saw him staring at her in astonishment did she realise what she must look like.

"It does not matter!" she said impatiently as if he had asked a question. "Just take me back. You shall have an... explanation of everything, and the money! It is all wonderful! Wonderful! But I must tell the *Comte* first."

"What must you tell him?" the Marquis asked.

Because he was not holding onto her, Trina was already halfway up the stairs.

"Come on!" she urged. "We cannot waste time in talking. I have to tell them! I must tell them!"

The Marquis realised as she finished speaking that she had disappeared and hurried after her.

When he reached the top Trina was still ahead of him and he followed her seeing that as she reached the end of the corridor, she intended to leave the Castle not by the front door but by the back.

He caught up with her as she was moving across the lawn, having slowed her pace a little because she was breathless.

"I suppose it is useless to ask you what all this is about?" he enquired.

"I cannot talk now . . . I have to get . . . back to the . . . Château!" Trina gasped.

As if he accepted the inevitable the Marquis was silent until the Château was just ahead of them.

"I told the *Comte* when he called for you," he said, "that you had already gone home and he should look for you in the garden."

She was still running although the Marquis managed to keep up with her by walking quickly, and Trina flashed him a smile.

"I guessed . . . that was . . . what you would . . . say."

Her fair hair was blowing in the warm wind, and with a dirty hand which left a smear of grey on her forehead, she swept it back.

The Marquis smiled but he said nothing, and a moment later Trina had reached the French windows leading into the Salon.

She rushed into the room to find as she had half-expected her mother and the *Comte* sitting on the sofa talking to each other.

At the sight of her they stared for a moment and the *Comte* jumped to his feet.

"Trina—what has—happened...?" Susi began.

"I have found it!" Trina cried. "I have found it... it is there in the dungeon... *Comte* Bernhard's treasure... where he must have hidden it all those years ago!"

She was so breathless from her long run that her words fell over each other and sounded almost incoherent.

She saw the expression of astonishment on the *Comte*'s face and said again:

"It is all there... the gold plate... a huge casket filled with... jewels... and bags... or what were once bags... of golden... coins!"

"The treasure?" the *Comte* questioned, but Susi moving towards Trina said:

"Dearest, what have you done to yourself? You are so dirty, but you are not hurt? Tell me you are not hurt?"

"No... Mama... I am not hurt... only excited because I have... found it for you... now you can get married . . . and live at the Castle . . . and stop . . . worrying!"

As she spoke she remembered for the first time since she had come into the Salon that the Marquis was standing behind her.

She turned round to see that he was just inside the window with a look in his eyes that it was impossible to interpret.

"His Lordship wants to know the . . . truth of what we have been doing," she said a little sarcastically. "I think we can now give him a very adequate . . . explanation . . . and there need be no further pretence."

"Yes, we must," Susi agreed. "I hated it anyway. But, dearest, you must wash and change. I cannot bear you to look like that."

"What does it matter?" Trina asked. "We have to go and get the treasure out so I shall only get dirty all over again."

She looked at the *Comte* but he was too dazed by what she had said to be able to express his feelings.

"What are we waiting for?" she asked. "You must come and see it!"

"Yes, what are we waiting for?" the *Comte* agreed as if he forced himself to speak calmly. "And as it happens the carriage is still at the door waiting instructions."

"Then quickly! Quickly!" Trina cried impatiently. "I want you to come and see what I have found . . . immediately, in case I have . . . imagined it."

She seized Susi by the hand as she spoke and pulled her across the room.

"Of course we want to come," Susi said, "but..."

As if the *Comte* suddenly entered into the spirit of the excitement, he cried:

"We are all going! How can we wait? If it is true, then it is the most fantastic thing that has ever happened!"

"It *is* true!" Trina declared.

She had reached the Hall and was drawing her mother towards the front door, when Susi said:

"My bonnet—I cannot go like this!"

"What does it matter, Mama?" Trina replied. "And if you touch the treasure... you will soon be as dirty as I am."

"We will all touch it," the *Comte* said firmly.

Trina had pulled Susi into the carriage and the *Comte* got in after them and was followed by the Marquis.

It was as if he was quite content to allow Trina to have her way, but Susi noticed as the carriage drove off, that his eyes were on Trina's face and she was aware of how disreputable her daughter looked.

She drew a small lace-edged handkerchief from her belt and bent forward to start wiping the dirt from Trina's face as she had done when she was a child.

Trina would have put up her hands to do it for herself, but Susi said quickly:

"No! Do not touch anything! You might at least

have stopped to wash your hands!"

Trina laughed.

"Oh, Mama, after all these centuries, does it really matter if my hands are clean or not? Think what this means to you. I can wash my hands for the next hundred years!"

Susi however continued to take the worst of the dirt from Trina's face, then she put the handkerchief into her hands.

"Perhaps this will be more effective," the Marquis suggested.

As he spoke he drew a large clean linen square from his pocket.

Trina smiled at him.

"I was trying to find a secret passage by which I could escape from you!"

"I wondered if there was one, when we heard how many the Castle contained," he replied. "But I thought it unlikely, as the dungeons are below ground."

"Who told you about the secret passages?" the *Comte* enquired.

"The servants have talked of nothing else ever since we arrived," the Marquis answered, "and actually I had read about your eccentric ancestor after I agreed to rent the Castle."

The *Comte* laughed.

"I had forgotten that you were likely to be a student of history."

The Marquis looked at Susi.

"Now I am beginning to understand why my mother was not told there was a second beautiful woman staying at the Château!"

The *Comte* laughed again.

"I see that among other talents you can add that of being a detective."

"I shall be interested to hear the whole story," the Marquis said, "but of course, after we have seen the treasure."

"That naturally comes first," the *Comte* replied.

Trina thought there was a slight acrimony between the two men. It did not surprise her when she remembered the scathing things the Marquis had said about the *Comte*.

She told herself that none of it mattered now.

She was sure that the treasure, because of its age, would be exceptionally valuable, and perhaps neither Jean, nor any future *Comtes* of Girone would have to marry a wife with a large dowry.

At the same time when they reached the Castle and Trina led the way back along the passages that led to the dungeons, she was just a trifle apprehensive.

Supposing after all, she had been mistaken and the treasure that was black with age was, in fact, worthless except for a few pieces which would be appreciated by a Museum?

She and the Marquis had left the door of the dungeons open and she ran down the steps and across the stone floor to the opening she had made in the wall.

"We can only go in one at a time," she said.

She looked at the *Comte* as she spoke.

"I claim my right of being the first," he replied with a smile.

"Of course!"

He took off his coat and put it on the floor and going down on his knees crawled through the opening, as Trina had done.

Susi picked up his coat and held it in her arms.

"It is cold and damp down here," she said. "Why did you come here in the first place?"

Trina's eyes twinkled and she looked at the Marquis.

"Are you prepared to explain to Mama," she asked, "why I was in the dungeon?"

"Certainly!" he replied. "I locked your daughter in here, Lady Sherington, because she refused to tell me the truth."

"You—locked Trina in the—dungeon?" Susi repeated in horrified tones. "How could you do—such a terrible thing?"

"I think perhaps you rather spoiled her when she was a child," the Marquis replied, "but now I see you together I am persuaded that she cannot be more than thirteen or fourteen!"

It took Susi a moment or two to realise he was paying her a compliment. Then she said:

"Trina is eighteen—but I do not like to think that you have been—unkind to her."

The Marquis smiled.

"You will understand, Lady Sherington," he said, "that as she was pretending to be you, I expected her to tell me the truth."

"I am sorry—very sorry," Susi said. "I knew we should never have done—such a thing—but I wanted to help—Jean—and also—although you may not believe it—to save your mother from that wicked and horrid man in Italy."

"What man in Italy?" the Marquis enquired.

Susi looked at Trina.

"Should I not have said that?"

"Yes, of course you can say it, Mama," Trina said. "I intended to tell His Lordship myself when the opportunity arose."

She saw the Marquis was waiting for an explanation and went on:

"Your mother told the Comte that if we did not find her the Elixir of Youth, she was going to leave here immediately to go to Rome and put herself in the hands of a man called Antonio di Casapellio who would have hypnotised and drugged her."

"I have heard of Casapellio," the Marquis said sharply. "But are you sure of what you are saying?"

"You can ask the Comte," Trina said. "Although what we have done may be reprehensible, we at least will not have harmed your mother physically, which is what I understand this Italian would do."

The Marquis was frowning.

Then before he could speak, there was a shout from the Comte and he appeared through the opening in the wall pushing in front of him a large casket.

It was the one Trina had seen amongst the other things and had opened it to see the jewels it contained.

The *Comte*'s white shirt was as dirty as Trina's gown, but he had managed to keep his face clean and as he got to his feet, he walked straight to Susi, put his arms around her and said:

"Tell me how soon you will marry me, my darling? For thanks to your daughter, I am now a very rich man!"

Chapter Seven

THE *Comte* raised his glass.

"To Trina!" he said, "and to our future happiness!"

He looked at Susi as he spoke, saw the expression in her eyes and thought he was the most fortunate man in the world.

He could still hardly believe it was true, that after all these centuries, *Comte* Bernhard's treasures should have been discovered at exactly the right moment.

While he had been prepared, because he loved Susi, to give up his Castle and a great many luxuries which he had thought were necessary to his comfort, he was aware that she, because she was so sensitive, would have always felt guilty.

Now everything would be perfect because he was well aware that what was lying at the moment on the dungeon floor had a value which was almost impossible to assess.

He had found it hard to believe when Trina had said that she had found the treasure, that it could in fact, be anything like as impressive as he hoped.

When he and the Marquis had taken it in turns to drag or push the pile through the narrow passage into the dungeon, every journey had made the *Comte* realise more fully the wonder of what Trina had discovered.

The de Girones might have guessed, he thought, that *Comte* Bernhard with his passion for concealed passages, staircases and secret chambers of one sort or another would have also contrived a secret place in which he could keep safely everything that was valuable in a time of war.

Although the history books had fulsome accounts of his magic, strangely enough there was little about his death.

In fact, the Girone family did not even know where he had died or how.

It might have been in battle, on one of his travels, or in the Castle itself.

Now the fact that there was so much treasure left in the Castle made the *Comte* think that perhaps his ancestor had been away from home when his life had come to an end.

But what was important at the moment was what he had concealed.

As the *Comte* and the Marquis passed the treasure through the hidden entrance, Susi and Trina took them and laid them out on the stone floor of the dungeon, and the piles of what they collected grew and grew.

Where Trina had seen one gold plate there were dozens. There were also goblets and flagons, bowls of every size, all of gold and ornamented with precious stones.

There were also other caskets like the large one which the *Comte* had brought out first, and they were not only masterpieces of fine craftsmanship, but contained jewellery mounted in gold and silver which he knew would be the delight and envy of every Museum in the country.

A large part of the value of what they had found was in the coins.

The bags in which *Comte* Bernhard had stowed them had crumbled into dust in the passing centuries and the *Comte* and the Marquis first of all tried to carry handfuls of them through the passage until Trina ran to collect something to contain them, from upstairs.

It was important, the *Comte* said, that nobody, for the moment, should know of their discovery.

She had therefore contented herself with snatching everything that seemed available in the nearest room, including two waste-paper baskets.

Then she had the bright idea that pillow-cases would be even more convenient as there was no chance of obtaining sacks.

She therefore went up to the nearest bedroom and pulled the cases from the pillows to carry four of them down to the dungeon in triumph.

Even then there were still quite a lot of coins which the *Comte* and the Marquis decided must wait until another day.

When they finally emerged, Susi gave an exclamation of horror at the *Comte*'s appearance while Trina laughed both at him and the Marquis.

"You look like a pair of blackamoors!" she said. "I cannot imagine what your valets will think you have been doing!"

"We shall have to think up some reasonable explanation," the *Comte* said. "But remember— not a word about the treasure in front of the servants."

"Are you afraid they might steal them?" Susi asked.

"My servants would never do such a thing," the *Comte* answered quickly, "but we could not prevent them talking. First the village would be agog with excitement, next reports in the newspapers would bring sightseers from all over France."

He smiled before he added:

"*Comte* Bernhard still remains a celebrity, at least in this part of the world."

"We will be very careful," Susi promised.

He smiled at her and she added:

"For Heaven's sake, let us go back and have baths. My hands are so dirty I am afraid to touch anything."

"Your gown is dirty too, Mama," Trina said, "but it has been in a good cause."

"A very good cause," the *Comte* agreed positively, "and I cannot remember ever being so happy in the whole of my life."

He was looking at Susi as he spoke and because she knew what his happiness meant her eyes met his. For a moment everything else was forgotten.

They walked from the dungeon and as the *Comte* locked the door carefully and put the key in his pocket, Trina felt that the Marquis was being left out of the excitement.

"I suppose," she began hesitatingly, "you . . . would not wish to . . . dine with . . . us tonight?"

As she spoke, she felt she was rather presuming on the *Comte*'s hospitality.

At the same time, if she was honest, she wanted the Marquis to be with them and she knew she was curious as to what he felt about her, now that he knew the truth of her deception.

"Of course you must dine with us!" the *Comte* agreed before the Marquis could speak. "I was, in fact, just about to invite Your Lordship. We have a lot of things to discuss."

"I shall be delighted to accept your invitation," the Marquis replied.

"We had better make dinner a little later than usual," the *Comte* went on, "it will take us some time to get clean."

When they drove away in the carriage which had been waiting for them, the *Comte* put out his hand, dirty though it was, to take Susi's.

"It does not seem possible that all these wonderful things have been hidden there for so long," she said. "Are they really as valuable as you hoped they would be, when Trina said she had found the treasure?"

"I cannot begin to estimate their worth," the *Comte* replied, "but that is unimportant beside the fact that we can be married immediately— tomorrow, if it can be arranged."

Susi gave a little cry.

"Tomorrow? But that is too soon!"

"Very well—the day after!" he conceded. "But I will wait no longer than that!"

Susi did not speak and Trina interposed to say:

"The *Comte* is right, Mama. There is no point in waiting. It will be lovely to know you need no longer worry about anything—except of course, your husband!"

She gave a mischievous little glance at the *Comte* who said quickly:

"If you are going to frighten Susi about my being a roué, I shall put you back in the dungeon and lock you in, as the Marquis did!"

"It was an unforgivable thing for him to do!" Susi cried indignantly. "How could you let him treat you in such a way?"

"I had very little choice," Trina answered.

She did not, however, wish to talk about what had happened between the Marquis and herself.

She was glad when the carriage arrived at the Château and she could run upstairs to her bedroom.

The maid who looked after her was horrified at the condition of her gown.

"What have you been doing, *M'mselle*?" she cried.

"We have been exploring the older parts of the Castle," Trina answered.

She did not say any more and the maid went away muttering that her expensive gown would never be the same.

Soaking in a warm bath scented with jasmine flowers, Trina thought with satisfaction that she had solved the problem she had set herself as to how to help her mother.

The only worry was a personal one—what she would do herself.

She obviously could not force herself, for the moment, on her mother and the *Comte*.

The one thing they would want on their honeymoon was to be alone, and she had no wish to return to England.

There her aunts would not only make her life miserable, but would be scandalised by the thought of her mother marrying so quickly after her father's death—and to a Frenchman!

She decided that at least for a little while she could stay with the *Duchesse*. After that, she would have to think again.

She could not help knowing that she would like more than anything else to get to know the Marquis better, but she had the uncomfortable feeling that he might think very differently.

No man likes being made a fool of, and he had been deceived by her pretence that she was an older and more sophisticated woman.

This, if nothing else, might make him decide that he was no longer interested in her, even as a sparring companion.

The idea was very dispiriting, and yet Trina could not help a little lift in her spirits because he was coming to dinner.

She chose what she was to wear with the greatest of care, changing her mind a dozen times, before she finally decided on a gown of white lace, so fine that it gave her an ethereal appearance, almost as if she was dressed by fairy hands.

The maid arranged her hair in a different manner from the style she had worn previously and instead of wearing jewels, she took a white camelia from a vase of them in her bedroom, and set it amongst the curls on top of her head.

"C'est charmant, M'mselle!" the maid exclaimed, and Trina could only hope that the Marquis would think so too.

When he arrived for dinner, she thought that no man could look more magnificent or more imposing in his evening-clothes.

But when he kissed Susi's hand in a conventional fashion and only bowed to her, she wondered apprehensively if he was still angry.

The dinner was a meal at which they all laughed and it was impossible to be gloomy about anything.

The *Comte* was in such high spirits and he and Susi were so happy that their excitement was infectious and Trina saw a different side to the Marquis than she had ever seen before.

He was witty and amusing and all through the meal he and the *Comte* tried to cap each other's stories.

Only when the servants had left the room did they talk of the subject which lay at the back of all their minds.

"What are you going to do about what lies on the dungeon floor?" the Marquis asked.

He was being discreet in not directly mentioning what was actually there and the *Comte* answered:

"I have already sent a telegram to the Curator of the Louvre, whom I know, asking him to come here with all possible speed. It will obviously take him a day or so."

He paused to look at Susi and say:

"You will not mind, my precious, if we start our honeymoon here?"

"I would not wish to be anywhere else," she said in a low voice and blushed as she spoke.

"I have been thinking," the Marquis said, "about your position now you are to be married, and I have a suggestion to make."

They all looked at him and he went on:

"I know that more than anything else that you will want to take your wife to your own Castle. I would therefore like, if it is at all possible, for my mother to move here to stay with your grandmother."

The *Comte* was obviously surprised and the Marquis went on:

"I have heard a great deal about *Madame la Comtesse* from the French Ambassador in London. His father, the *Marquis* de Vallon, was I understand, in love with her for many years."

"Of course!" the *Comte* interposed. "I remember my grandmother speaking of him and I think I also met him."

"His son speaks of your grandmother as one of the most interesting as well as the most beautiful women, he has ever seen."

The Marquis paused before he went on:

"I have not met the *Comtesse*, but I cannot help thinking, from all I have heard, that she is just the sort of person who might help and influence my mother at this particular moment in her life."

"That is a marvellous idea!" Susi exclaimed.

"Perhaps," the Marquis continued, "if she could see how another woman, as beautiful as she was, has not only accepted old age gracefully, but has also been exceedingly brave about her disability, I think there would be no further need for her to seek the assistance of quacks and crooks."

"Which we tried to be," the *Comte* said

frankly. "And that reminds me—I forgot this in all the excitement."

As he spoke, he drew from the inside pocket of his evening-coat a cheque which he passed across the table to the Marquis.

"If it is made out in your name," the Marquis said, "I would like you to endorse it."

The *Comte* looked surprised and he explained:

"I intend to cash it and keep the money for the moment, so that my mother will not have so much to spend. I am also determined that whatever happens, I will not allow her to get into the clutches of someone like Casapellio or anyone else who will extract large sums from her."

"I am afraid it might be a somewhat difficult task," the *Comte* remarked.

"I realise that I have been at fault in the past," the Marquis said, "because I left her alone and did not provide her, as I should have done, with the right sort of companions."

"I think loneliness might have had something to do with it," the *Comte* said.

"That is what I must prevent in the future," the Marquis answered, "therefore I would like, if you will permit me, and if the *Comtesse* will agree, her to stay here."

"I am sure that can be arranged," the *Comte* replied. "When I told *Grand'mère* this evening what had happened she was so excited that she is determined tomorrow to inspect the treasure for herself."

"I thought she would be pleased," Susi said.

"She is even reconciled to my marrying an Englishwoman without a large dowry," the *Comte* said with a smile.

"You are—sure?"

Susi's question made him put out his hand towards her as he said:

"Quite, quite sure. *Grand'mère* loves me, and I told her with considerable eloquence that I could never be happy without you."

"Oh—Jean . . . !"

Susi could hardly breathe the words, but they were very moving.

"Will you speak to your grandmother tonight?" the Marquis asked, as if he wished to get everything settled.

"But of course. I promised her anyway that Susi and I will say good-night to her after dinner."

"Did you invite her to join us?" Susi questioned.

"Of course I did," he replied, "but she was so excited by what had happened that I think the effort of getting up and dressed would have been too much. But she insisted on a glass of champagne with which to drink our health!"

"I am sure your grandmother is often lonely too," Trina remarked. "It must be very hard when one has been the centre of admiring friends, to be alone, even in a place as beautiful as this."

"I am quite certain," the *Comte* smiled, "that

Grand'mère and the Marchioness will find a great many interests in common, and as His Lordship has said, in future we must see that they have the right sort of friends to keep them amused and happy."

It flashed through Susi's mind that what every elderly lady really wanted was grandchildren who would occupy both their thoughts and hours of their time.

As she met the *Comte*'s eyes she knew he was thinking the same thing and it made her feel shy.

She looked so adorable that his fingers tightened on her hand which he still held.

There was no need for words. They were so closely attuned to each other that they vibrated to each other's thoughts as if to music.

"As we have finished dinner, I think we should go to your Grandmother now," Susi said. "It is growing late."

She rose as she spoke and as she and Trina left the Dining-Room, the gentlemen followed them.

Susi walked up the stairs beside the *Comte*, his arm round her waist, and Trina went into the Salon tinglingly aware that the Marquis had followed her and they were now alone.

She walked to the window to look out onto the dusk of the night.

It was very warm, the faint wind there had been earlier in the day had gone and now there was a stillness, as if even the earth had stopped breathing.

Unexpectedly, the Marquis took Trina's hand in his and drew her through the window and onto the lawn.

She did not speak, but his clasp was firm and she thought there was something determined about him which made her quiver.

The stars were glittering overhead and the moon turned the Castle to silver so that it looked as if it had stepped out of a fairy-story and into their dream.

The Marquis drew Trina towards the cypress trees and she knew he was going to the place above the river where they had listened to the nightingales.

Only when they reached it did he release her hand and she stood where she had stood that first night when he had joined her and she had thought he was the *Comte*.

She did not look at him but at the river below shimmering in the light of the moon, the country beyond it undulating away into the darkness of the horizon.

It was then she heard very faintly in the distance the trilling note of a nightingale.

She held out her hand, just as she had done that first evening, to warn the Marquis not to speak. Then as the birds seemed to come nearer she felt as if she had stepped back into the past.

What had happened then was happening again, and yet in the days between so much had occurred that she felt almost as if she had lived a lifetime of emotions.

One nightingale was singing; and now as if it was inevitable it was joined by another, and they sang in unison.

The sound was so exquisite, so moving, that without even meaning to, Trina turned her head to look at the Marquis and see what he was feeling.

He was nearer to her than she expected, his eyes were on her face, and as she looked up at him he said very quietly, almost beneath his breath:

"A song of love, my lovely one, and that was what I was waiting to hear."

At the term of endearment Trina's eyes widened for a moment, then without realising what she was doing, she was in his arms.

She felt his lips take possession of hers and she knew this was what she had been waiting for, what she had been longing for and what she had been afraid of losing.

His kiss swept her up into the sky as it had done before, only now it seemed even more insistent, more wonderful and more ecstatic than it had been.

She felt her heart beating against the Marquis's and she knew as he drew her closer and still closer that as their bodies merged into each other's, so did their hearts and minds.

She was his, and she surrendered herself completely to the power and dominance of him because she had no resistance left.

Now there was not only the song of the nightingales, but Trina felt as if there was the music of the angels singing not in her ears, but in her heart, and the rapture the Marquis gave her, was part of the stars, the moon and God Himself.

The Marquis raised his head.

"I love you!"

Because it was impossible to speak Trina turned her face against his shoulder.

"I fell in love with you," he went on, "when I first came through the cypress trees and saw you looking up at the sky and thought you were too beautiful to be human."

"You . . . really do . . . love me?"

"I love you until you fill my world and there is nothing else but you, but I am in fact, at the same time—angry!"

"Angry?" she whispered. "Because I deceived you?"

"Not with your magic tricks," he replied, "they are immaterial, but because you led me to believe that you were your mother, and I believed that she belonged to the *Comte*."

"And that . . . upset you?"

"So much so," the Marquis replied, "that after I kissed you, I decided I would never see you again!"

"Oh . . . no!"

It was a cry of horror as Trina remembered how much she had wanted to see him.

"When I left the day before yesterday for Monte Carlo, I decided I would not return to the Castle as I had intended."

Trina drew in her breath.

"How could you have thought of anything so... cruel when I was... longing to see you again?"

"How was I to know that?" the Marquis asked. "I thought you were just a very lovely, flirtatious woman, wishing to have every man she met, at her feet, and I had no wish to add to their number."

"There is... no-one."

"Then I was right—nobody has kissed you except me?"

"No... no!"

"Oh, my darling, you do not know how I fought against believing what my instinct told me. Are you surprised that I am angry?"

"Please... forgive me."

He looked down at her eyes pleading with his, thinking in the moonlight, she was so beautiful, that he would impress this moment on his mind forever.

Then as if he realised that her beauty was not only ethereal but very human, his lips sought hers again and he kissed her until the world seemed to swing dizzily round them and they were both breathless.

The Marquis drew Trina towards the stone seat on which they had sat before.

She sat down with his arms around her and with a little sigh of sheer happiness, her head fell back against his shoulder.

"Now we will make plans," he said. "If your

mother and de Girone are to be married the day after tomorrow, I suggest we are married tomorrow evening."

"T . . . tomorrow?" Trina exclaimed in sheer astonishment.

"Why not?" the Marquis asked. "But because we are in France it will have to be a Civil ceremony first, in front of the Mayor, then I imagine there is an English Church of some sort in Arles."

"That is very . . . soon!"

"What else are you suggesting we should do without your mother to chaperon you? I can hardly believe you intend to spend her honeymoon with her?"

"No . . . of course not," Trina replied. "I was actually planning I would go to Paris and stay with the *Duchesse* d'Aubergue. She did, in fact, ask me to."

The Marquis's arms tightened.

"And you imagine I would allow you to do that?"

Trina gave him a questioning little smile and he laughed.

"All right—I am jealous—madly jealous! That is why I intend to marry you now and at once, before I lose you."

"You need not be . . . afraid of . . . doing that."

"How can I be sure?" he asked. "I am not sure of anything where you are concerned. You have taunted me, teased me, and fought me in a manner I found extremely irritating, and at the same time, quite enchanting!"

His lips were near to hers as he added:

"I want you! I want you as I have never wanted anything in my whole life, and I love you as I never thought it possible to love any woman. You are mine, Trina, and I do not intend to wait!"

There was a determination in his voice which made Trina thrill to the mastery of him.

She knew that however much she prevaricated she would, in the end, do exactly as he wanted not only now, but for the rest of her life.

He was the conqueror, the victor, the type of man she had always admired. Someone she might coax to get her own way, but who otherwise would always be her master.

At the same time, Trina knew it would be fun to be with him, fun to make him fight for what he wanted, and even more marvellous and exciting when she finally surrendered.

"Supposing," she asked in a small voice, "I prefer to have a . . . grand wedding? After all, you are of great . . . importance in England. Your friends would expect that we should be married in St. George's, Hanover Square, with at least two pages and ten bridesmaids, besides a Reception for five hundred guests."

"Then they will be disappointed," the Marquis said firmly, "and so will you! I am not taking you back to England until I am sure that you love me as much as I love you, and I need no longer be afraid of letting you out of my sight."

"And . . . where are you . . . suggesting we should go for our . . . honeymoon?"

She knew even as she asked the question, that he had already planned it.

"My yacht arrived at Marseilles today, on its way to Monte Carlo," he answered. "I have telegraphed the Captain to have everything ready for our arrival!"

"You were quite ... confident I would ... agree to ... marry you?"

"If you refuse I can always lock you in the dungeon again until you agree!"

Trina gave a little laugh, then she said:

"I was trying so hard to escape so that when you unlocked the door, you would find nobody there and would be puzzled as to what had happened to me."

"I would still have caught you again," the Marquis said. "You can never escape me! I knew that even while I tried to leave."

"Would you ... really have ... stayed away and ... forgotten me?" Trina asked in a low voice.

"If I tell the truth—no!" the Marquis replied. "I knew when I spent a sleepless night in an Hotel at Nice before I caught the earliest train possible back to Arles, that I had to see you again. Had you belonged to a thousand *Comtes*, I would still have made you mine."

As if the fear that she might have belonged to some other man still frightened him, he put his fingers under her chin and turned her face up to his.

Then he kissed her fiercely, possessively, de-

mandingly, in a different way from the kisses he
had given her before.

Only when his passion became so tempestuous
that Trina gave a little murmur of protest and
put up her hands as if to protect herself did he
set her free.

The fire in his eyes was unmistakable and
when he looked at her, he said, his voice very
deep and a little unsteady:

"Forgive me, my darling. I love you so wildly,
so overwhelmingly that I forget how young you
are, and how, although you pretend to be otherwise—inexperienced."

"Will . . . will that . . . bore you?"

"I will find it very exciting, so exciting in fact
that you must not allow me to frighten you."

He pulled her close to him, but more gently.

"Oh, my darling, you are everything I looked
for in a wife, but thought I would never find."

"Are you . . . sure about . . . that?"

"I thought young girls were gauche, stupid
and with no brains. I was wrong."

He moved his lips gently against her skin as
he went on:

"I thought I wanted sophistication and a
woman who had a knowledge of the world, and
again I was wrong. What I want is you, every
precious scrap of you, to be mine now and for
all eternity."

Trina put her arm around his neck and drew
his head down to hers.

"That is what . . . I want too," she whispered. "I want to . . . belong to you. I want to make you . . . happy. Please . . . please teach me about love . . . so that you will . . . not be . . . disappointed."

"I will never be that," the Marquis answered, "and teaching you about love, my precious one, will be the most thrilling and wonderful thing I have ever done in my life."

He was kissing her again, not so fiercely, but at the same time demandingly, as if he wooed her with his kisses, and Trina thought that not only her whole body responded to what he wanted of her, but her heart, her mind and her soul.

Vaguely, somewhere far away, she heard the nightingales singing and she thought as they sang they were soaring high into the sky.

Only now she and the Marquis were flying with them towards the stars, and the light and the glory of it made them too, part of a song of love.

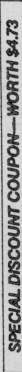